Hard Ride to Glory

Griffin Boone is happy in his Wyoming valley; he has his Arrowhead ranch, his close friends, a good stock of cattle and a job as a part time deputy sheriff in the county of Liberty. Boone has ridden through the battlefields of the Civil War, served throughout with John Bell Hood's Texas Brigade, he has survived the horror of battle and found peace and solitude with a woman and a shared past. That long ago trail they once unknowingly rode draws them ever closer together until their lives are threatened by Heck Thomas and his outlaw crew of gunfighters and vagabond thieves. Ride with Boone from the peaceful town of Liberty to the ruins of Glory, a ghost town in the foothills of the Big Horn Mountains where past meets present in a blaze of gunfire. Griffin Boone is a quiet, unassuming man, a gentleman – but make no mistake, you cross him at your peril. . . .

Hard Ride to Glory

Harry Jay Thorn

A Black Horse Western

ROBERT HALE

ISBN 978-0-7198-2035-9

The Crowood Press
The Stable Block
Crowood Lane
Ramsbury
Marlborough
Wiltshire SN8 2HR

www.crowood.com

Robert Hale is an imprint
of The Crowood Press

Typeset by
Derek Doyle & Associates, Shaw Heath
Printed and bound in Great Britain by
CPI Group (UK) Ltd, Croydon, CR0 4YY

To friends and western fans everywhere, thank you for reading, saddle up and help keep the genre alive.

PROLOGUE

Horace Jennings rolled out of his warm single bed at seven-fifteen sharp. He washed, shaved, made toast, scrambled three eggs and washed the food down with a mug of dark coffee. He then made himself a lunch pail of fruit and sandwiches neatly wrapped in greaseproof paper before shedding his dressing gown and slipping into his light-coloured summer-wear pants and white cotton shirt. Brushing his thinning grey hair crossways so as to cover as much of his shiny pate as possible, a vain man, he examined himself carefully in the fly-speckled dressing table mirror before pulling the elasticated black sleeve protectors over his shirt and slipping his tinted eye shade on to his pink forehead. Satisfied that all was in order he left his little apartment above the general store and walked the short distance to the small sub post office of which he was king. The Chicago morning air was laced with the stink of cattle and although the stock pens that surrounded the area were empty due to the passing of the spring roundup, the smell of the beasts lingered long into the summer.

After passing the time of day with Howie Davis, the telegrapher, in his office next to the post office he unlocked the door and entered his kingdom. It was a routine he had followed for much of the past twelve years of his life. It was exactly seven fifty-five. You could set your pocket watch by Horace Jennings.

Once inside, he carefully locked the door behind him and opening the side gate, he went behind the counter and checked he had everything to hand. He always did. He checked the cash in the money box, $45 and some small change, he then checked that the rubber stamp pad was sufficiently charged with ink and finally unlocked the small safe which, apart from a fully charged but elderly Remington cap and ball .44 pistol given to him by his father, a veteran of the Civil War, the safe only contained a box of US Mail seals and a stack of important federal mail which had reached him on the previous day – but too late for delivery to the court house.

As the post office clock chimed, loudly declaring the arrival of the eighth hour of the morning, he released the noisy door blind and undid the lock before returning to his position behind the counter to await either the first customer of the day or the delivery of the local newspaper.

He did not have to wait very long. At five past the hour, two men entered the post office. They were dirty, dressed in soiled clothing, there was a smell to them, unwashed, he guessed homeless and sleeping rough; there were many such men in Chicago, the bulk of them to be found living close to the tracks of the North

Western Railway. Some were characters in their own right, harmless, even interesting at times and grateful for a small handout. Others were not so pleasant and to be avoided, even making eye contact with some was a risk. This pair fell into the latter category. The younger of the two was a teenager but even young rattlesnakes have a nasty bite. Horace felt an immediate sense of foreboding as the larger of the two men approached the counter, studied him for a moment and then pulled a revolver from the deep confines of his soiled overcoat and pointing it directly at the trembling postal worker said, 'No noise, old man, no heroics, just open the tin box and pass me the money.'

Horace knew the drill, his life was more important to the US Mail Service than was a few dollars. He opened the box and handed the $45 to the big man, holding up the tin box to show him it was empty. The man looked at the small bundle of notes in his dirty hand and then back at Jennings, an expression of disappointment mixed with disbelief on his grimy face. He looked past the trembling man, his dark eyes fixed upon the small safe, smiling then. 'Open the safe and bring me the cash from in there.'

'The safe is empty save for a few legal documents and. . . .'

'Shut your lying mouth and bring it me.'

'Yes, sir.' Horace muttered the words, knowing full well what he was going to do and wishing he wasn't. It was a matter of pride, the post office was in a poor area of the city but it had never been robbed and he had no wish for it to happen for the first time on his watch. He turned, knelt down and slowly opened the safe door, pulled out the Remington, turned and fired it on the up. A loud click, a misfire. He stared down at the useless weapon and then up at the big man, their eyes meeting as the gun in the man's hand belched flame and black smoke, the round taking him in the shoulder, knocking him back and into the wall, sliding down to a sitting position, the fear coupled with a dim realization that he could hear a police whistle in the distance, the screaming voice of Howie Jones, then those too fading. Another shot and more pain as the growing darkness closed around him.

Ten minutes later the two men were squatting in an empty freight wagon, sitting on dried cow dung and straw as the big engine pulled out of the stock yards and headed westwards on its long return journey back to cattle country.

CHAPTER ONE

WAGON WHEELS

It looked like being a fine day, at least it started out that way as bad days often do. I saddled the grey mare, checked my canteen, called into the cook shack to tell Henry Mendoza I would be out for most of the day then headed south with the sun on my left and the Big Horn Mountains still wearing their winter snow caps behind me. A balmy spring day, the long pale grass buzzing with insects and dotted with bright scarlet Indian paintbrush, the flowers reminding me of blood splashes on a yellow dress. An odd thought. I had county papers to serve and knew my arrival would be welcomed by some recipients and resented by others but it was a job, part-time, but still $3 a day and it helped me pass the long and often empty hours. The cattle carrying my Arrowhead brand did not need my attention and were safe in the hands of the small crew that worked the ranch for me. My last call, getting on for mid-afternoon, was to Heck Thomas and his two-by-four spread, the Half Moon, a small ranch but ideally situated on the banks of Liberty Creek. I offered to buy it from him on many occasions but, understandably, he was reluctant to part with it. At near on eighty years old he asked me once, where the hell would he go? Certainly not to Liberty; he knew he would never be able to cope with town life even though it was the county seat, a large and comfortable enough place to live. He took the papers from me and complained that with the federal taxes and now having the county's served on him he was wondering just who he was working for, himself or the government in one guise or another. I told him I agreed with him but that was the way it was. Unconvinced, he wondered why I was delivering notices for $3 a day when I had such a fine ranch of my own and I pointed out, as I had done on countless occasions before, that I needed to make money to pay my taxes just the same as he did. He was never going to be convinced of that being the reason and he was right; I did it because I enjoyed doing it and being a part-time deputy did have a sunny side, part of which was that I got see him every few months and partake of his home-made brew, a moonshine that would brighten any man's day. He asked me to stay for supper but I told him, no, I had to head back after checking a boundary line just to the south of his place but that I would call back the following week for a drink and maybe stay over the night. That pleased the old man greatly; he had a fear of dying alone in the front yard and being eaten by a bear. I told him a bear big enough and tough enough to eat him had not been seen in Liberty County in years.

But I understood his worry, his loneliness, and told him so.

'How long have you been alone now, Griff?' he asked me, standing there on the veranda of his little ranch house in his faded red long johns, sucking on an empty corncob pipe, darkened and stained from years of usage.

'Around ten years now I guess.' Was it really that long ago? That old familiar tug of sadness. . . .

'She was a lovely lady, God knows what she saw in you though.'

'Sometimes wonder about that myself, Heck, I surely do.'

The old man smiled. 'I guess you're not all bad for a lawman.'

'Part-time lawman.' I swung back aboard the mare. 'See you soon, Heck, I will send one of the hands for a ride by once in a while to check on you but do not give them any of that 'shine, they are far too young.'

'How come you never told any of the federals about my still?'

'I wanted to right enough, but the sheriff wouldn't hear of it, said it's the best damned stuff he ever tasted, asked me to bring a jug back with me next time I visit.'

'You tell Joe Sawyer, he wants it, he comes and gets it.'

He was chuckling to himself as I rode out of his front yard and headed south again toward the long valley that bisected my land almost in the centre. Ten minutes later I reached the lower end of Liberty Creek, a lively run off from the North Platte, and paused there on the brow of a low hill that looked down over the flatlands below.

There was unexpected activity down in the trees by the creek, a small covered wagon with its two-mule team tethered to the one of the aspens and a little further on two saddle horses tied off to a fallen tree, long ago stripped of its bark by the winter winds.

The wagon was down on the right rear axle and the big wheel lying flat on the grass. A man and a boy were standing close together. I took out my army field glasses and took a closer look. The man was actually a woman in dungarees and baggy plaid shirt, her hair mostly hidden by a broad-brimmed straw hat. The boy, about ten I guessed, was close by her side holding her hand. I could not figure it at first then a man stepped out from behind the wagon followed closely by another, a much shorter man; both wore a sidearm. They were unshaven, the bigger man in a battered derby, his companion in a chequered cap. Both were poorly dressed, ragged and dirty town clothes, drifters with no place to go and no hurry to be there. It was not really any of my business but they were on my land so I gently touched the big mare with my heels and pushed her down to the creek.

I reined in a few yards from the wagon, touched the brim of my hat to the woman and ignoring the two men asked, 'Anything I can do to help, ma'am?' She looked pleased, almost relieved to see me.

'No, nothing you can do, we got it covered.' A hard-edged eastern voice clear of any really noticeable accent, a hint of Irish maybe, a clipped speech pattern. It was the larger of the two men, stepping clear of the wagon and taking a couple of steps in my direction. He was big, over six foot, stubble-covered face with a large

14

hooked nose, swollen with either too much booze or too many barroom brawls.

'That wheel needs a new iron,' I observed, keeping my voice low but directing my words at the woman. 'It is going to need a blacksmith and he will not be riding out here today, but I can send him out or get the wheel taken to Liberty in the morning if you would like me to.'

'I told you, mister, we got it covered.' The larger man again.

'That right, lady?' I said. 'Do you believe they have it covered?'

'Mind your own goddamned business.' A squeaky voice, it was the smaller of the two men, the one in the battered cap, long blond hair, unshaven narrow pallid cheeks, down-at-heel boots.

'Well, I suppose I could mind my own business but you are on my land so that kind of makes this very much my business. Now, you let the lady talk, I want anything from either of you I will ask you directly.' I softened my voice and turned to the woman. 'You want I should ride on, just say so.'

'No, we would like your help.' There was a quiet desperation in her voice.

'I told you twice, mister, I will not tell you again.' The big man reached for his gun as he spoke. I drove the big mare straight at him; a powerful horse, her shoulder struck him full on, flooring him, knocking him sideways with considerable force, the drawn weapon falling from his hand. His companion was reaching for his sidearm as I pulled and capped a round over his head. He dropped the gun, sank to his knees with his hands above

15

his head yelling, 'Don't shoot, mister, please don't shoot me.' I could see that beneath the oversized clothes, the dirt and grime, he was just a kid – maybe fifteen years old or so.

'Not today, son, you pick up those pistols and hand them to me butt-first and you be very careful about it.' He did as he was told, handed me the two revolvers, blued steel Colt Frontiers, both in .45 calibre and in poor condition. I opened the loading gate of each one and emptied their cylinders of shells, dropping the rounds into the long grass and tossing the empty guns at his feet. 'Now you get those two horses, you take this piece of trash with you and you ride clear of my property. I see you again I will do you harm.' I could see he had registered the star on my chest.

'Yes sir, sheriff, we be gone.' He helped the dazed man to his feet and pitifully tried to dust him down.

The big man pushed him away and glared up at me. 'We are not alone out here and we will not forget this day.'

'Good, maybe you did learn something from it then.'

'I didn't mean it that way, I meant. . . .'

'I know what you meant, dumb ass, remember it for whatever reason best pleases you but do remember it. Now you ride a half hour from here in any direction and you will be clear of my property, that will make me happy and if I am happy, you are happy. You ever want to see me you be sure to ask for me in Liberty, most folk know me there, just ask for Griffin Boone. Now, get along.'

'What about our guns?'

'Pick them up and leather them fast.'

I rode behind them to the edge of the willows and watched the oddly matched pair ride through the trees and beyond the creek until they were just two spots on the open prairie, then out of sight hidden by a rise. When I rode back to the broken wagon the woman and the boy were exactly as I had left them.

I could see that the woman was still holding the trembling boy close. The youngster was the first to speak, his voice husky, and his eyes tear-filled. 'You really the sheriff, mister?'

'No, son, just a deputy, Griffin Boone, and you are. . . ?'

He did not answer, simply stared at me, confused and frightened.

'His name is Chuck, Charlie Otis, I'm Laura Otis and we are on our way south.' The woman answered my question for him.

'Alone?'

'We had a guide but he left us a couple of days ago, ran off with our milk cow, my rifle and Chuck's pony. He was a very disagreeable man.'

'When did that pair join you?'

'Two, maybe three hours before you came along – they said they could help if I fed them, which I did.'

'Did they say where they were from?'

'No, not from, but said they were headed for a town called Glory.'

I smiled. 'Well, one way or another they should be happy there.'

'You know it?'

17

'Yes I know of it.' I changed the subject. 'Did they harm you in any way, you or the boy?'

'No but they scared Chuck, I can look after myself, I still have a knife.'

Was that a warning to me, I wondered? She was feisty and confident and yet she had welcomed my intervention, perhaps she recognized the odds of two to one were stacked against her and just having me to deal with halved those odds. Maybe, but she had looked relieved at seeing the Liberty County badge on my vest.

'You don't have a man with you, a husband?' I asked.

'No, my husband was killed in the war but I have a little money, I can pay you if you are able to help us get the wagon mended.'

'Where exactly are you headed?'

'Texas.'

'That is a long hard way from here.'

'The journey will be worth the hardship.'

'You must have one big reason for wanting gone.' I knew I was prying, but it was my nature to seek answers to things I did not fully understand and it was difficult for me to comprehend the reason for making such a long and hazardous trek with only a boy, a rifle, a knife and a milk cow.

'We want a new life, my husband fought for the south – we were not welcome in the north. We have moved on many occasions.'

'The war has been over a long time.'

'For some a long time is not long enough.' It was an explanation of sorts and probably all I was going to get there and then.

18

I let it go, her voice was strong but overburdened by some greater hidden inner sadness, tired, weary perhaps of a great many things. She was an attractive woman, not lovely but handsome in a mannish way, tall, auburn hair peeping out from under her hat but the weariness seemed to have invaded every part of her being. Tired, shoulders now slumped, no laughter lines, just crow's feet around hazel eyes.

I dismounted and ground-hitched the mare to the discarded wheel and turned my attention to the frightened boy, getting down one knee – I find it better to talk to kids at eye level, not looking down on them or having them look up to me. It was something I had learned as a lawman, wearing a badge is not all about fast draws and outlaws. I held out my hand after first removing my leather glove. 'Good to meet you, Chuck, do you have a hat? You need a hat out here in the sun.' He nodded, looked up at his mother for reassurance and nervously took my outstretched hand. I held it there for a moment. 'Don't worry about those men, Chuck, they will not come back, they will not hurt you. I promise you while you are under my protection, nothing bad will happen to you.'

Those simple reassuring words would come back to haunt me in the weeks to come but there and then they stiffened the boy's back and his grip on my hand tightened. I smiled at him, got to my feet and nodding to his mother I set to examining the broken wheel. It was repairable but would need a hot forge and a blacksmith's hammer to fix it and that could not be organized until the morning. 'I will need to take the wheel into the blacksmith's in Liberty but not tonight. One of my men will pick it up in a buckboard tomorrow and take it into town. It will be a couple of days or so. In the meantime, you cannot stay out here, I don't believe those scavengers will be back but you never can tell, they may lick their wounds and decide to give me a try.' I smiled at the kid. 'Get the mules, son, you and your mother are coming back to Arrowhead with me, rest up while the wagon is fixed and I will see if I can set you up with another guide, at least to the border. How does that sound to you, ma'am?'

'I don't know what to say. Thank you sounds so, so. . . .' Her voice trailed off.

'It sounds good enough to me. Now, it's an hour's ride and we can just about make it before dark. Pack a bag for whatever you need, any valuables, change of clothes, allow for three days at the most.'

I watched the woman and the boy quickly packing a few precious belongings into a couple of gunny sacks and awkwardly mounting the bare-backed mules, not realizing for a moment what train of events I had set into motion or how many lives, including my own, would be affected by that one broken wagon wheel.

CHAPTER TWO

THE GLORY HOLE

James Treadwell and Huck Flynn rode hard out of the valley; they paused once, looking back toward the stand of big willows that bordered Liberty Creek. Huck looking back, fighting his horse, the big man spitting, swearing, fancied he could see the damned lawman watching them from the rise but he could not be sure, it may have been the long shadows that promised the coming of evening and a long night on the trail back to where the rest of the bunch had gathered. Not being familiar with the trail and worried about getting lost in the darkness of a moonless night, Flynn ordered that they make camp in a small aspen wood just off the trail leading to Glory and cook up some of the last of the white tail he had shot and dressed several days earlier. Treadwell was only sixteen years old, he packed a gun and could shoot it pretty well and would no doubt, if the need arose, put down a man with it but he still had that

21

childish fear of the dark and he was more than happy that they make camp and build a fire which would push some of that darkness away from him. He gathered as much wood and kindling as possible in the last of the evening light, which finally gave way to the rich velvety darkness of the Wyoming night.

'I figured we were on to something good there had that badge not shown up, that mare damned near killed me.'

Huck was still irritable about the incident by the creek, he had been bitching about it most of the late afternoon, aiming the words at Treadwell like it was his fault.

'She didn't have no money, you can't eat mules and the kid kept on crying, I think we are better off out of it.'

'Maybe she could have paid me in some other way, fine looking woman.'

'Don't go talking like that, Huck, they do not take kindly to folk who harm women out here, not like back home.'

'Cow chasers, shit kickers and clod hoppers on their high and mighty horses – we would soon cool their asses back in Chi.' Huck missed Chicago, he missed the buildings, the bars, the stockyards, the women. Had he not killed a teller in the post office they had robbed, had the man not been stupid enough to take a hideaway out of a safe, they would have made it but instead they fled west just ahead of the law and had been down on their luck ever since. Still, that would soon be behind them, their fortunes would change when they reached Glory and met up with Ben Logan and the rest of the old gang. Logan would see them right. He thought about that as he chewed on the half-cooked meat and warm beans the kid had prepared for their supper. Dumb kid but still, he was company. '*Don't shoot me, please don't shoot me,*' as if the old bastard would have and besides you never give up your piece, no way – words will not deter a man who is bent on shooting you.

'What do you think Glory will be like, Huck? Good food, maybe a bed?' Treadwell interrupted his train of thought. His voice was eager; if he had a tail, Flynn thought, it would be wagging. How the hell would he know what Glory was like? All he had was a map and a piece of crumpled paper with some scrawled directions on it.

'Whatever it is, kid, it will be home for a while. Now keep the fire burning, it will keep the wild animals away.'

'What sort of wild animals would be out here, Huck?'

'Oh, a bear or maybe a mountain lion I shouldn't wonder. Get some sleep, we will start out early and should be in town by late morning.' He smiled to himself in the darkness, knowing he had planted a seed and that the kid would be keeping the fire burning all night lest the beasts he saw in the moving shadows thrown there by the flickering light of the fire devour him.

The pair reached the crest of the rock-strewn rise around about midday, the riders almost as weary as the horses they were riding. If he had read the map correctly, Glory would be over that crest.

'Jesus H. Christ!' A whispered exclamation as Flynn looked down on what was left of the township of Glory. A ghost town, an overgrown street littered with tumbleweed and sagebrush; the buildings, such as they were, long past their glory days – if the settlement had ever acquired such a standing. There were no great gold rushes in Wyoming but here and there trace gold was found and mined until, as with Glory, the vein came to an end and the small creek running behind the decaying buildings had given up its meagre supply of dust. Only one dilapidated building showed any semblance of real shelter. The saloon, its faded sign declaring it rather grandly to have been the Glory Hole Saloon – a name, a promise it never could have lived up to fulfilling. There were five horses tied off at the hitching rail and a trickle of smoke drifting out of a rusted metal chimney running up the near side of the building. 'Not quite what I expected, kid, not what I expected at all.' He kneed his mount forward and down the narrow pass followed by Treadwell, a look of disappointment clear on his dirty young face.

Their approach was not challenged and dismounting they tied their horses to the hitching rail, ignoring the snorts of welcome from the mounts already tied there.

The man stepped clear of the alleyway running alongside the decrepit building, lowering the sawed-off twelve gauge he was carrying and addressing Flynn. 'You sure enough took your sweet time getting here, Flynn, who's the kid?'

'Jimmy Treadwell, he rides with me.'

'Saw you coming down the cut, there is an easier way down.'

'I only had the map Logan sent me, Lomax, he's not the best cartographer in the damned world. What is this godforsaken place?'

Chad Lomax ignored the question, asking one of his own. 'Cartographer?'

'A word I picked up somewhere. He inside?'

'Yes, we liberated some booze from a small town outside of Laramie. You are the last to arrive, Smitty and Harris are in there along with a new kid, a friend of Logan's.'

Flynn nodded and pushed open the batwing doors which creaked and groaned on their rusted hinges. It was gloomy inside, two men at the bar turned and nodded but the dark man sitting just inside the door playing solitaire with a dog-eared pack of red Bicycles did not look up, staring down at the cards and asking in a lazy south-of-the-line voice, 'You must be Huck Flynn, I hear you had to flee Chicago with the law on your back.'

'We did not flee, we rode out after a job went sour on us.'

'You killed a civilian in cold blood for nothing, you have a yellow streak a mile wide, you bring that with you?' The man did not look up from his cards.

'Who the hell are you, you goddamned 'breed, best you watch your mouth around me.'

The man got to his feet, raised his head, handsome, swarthy, black moustache over a broad upper lip, smiling from a white-toothed mouth. He wore a cross-draw rig with a stainless steel Colt settled easily in the tan leather.

Flynn let his long coat fall open, his hand raised above his own sidearm.

'That will do, the both of you stand down.' The voice was cold, a touch of the Irish, the words softly spoken but not to be ignored. 'You know the rules, Flynn, no fighting among the bunch, save that for those who would do us harm.' He turned to the long bar, the rough pine planks standing on empty barrels, and poured himself a generous shot of amber liquid from a stone jug. A tall, handsome man dressed entirely in black, a Texas Stetson on his head, dark red hair poking out from beneath the brim, matching the colour of the three-day growth on his sunburned face. If he was wearing a gun it was not visible.

'The 'breed started it, Ben, I was only going to finish it.'

'We don't use that terminology here, Huck. That is Emilio Vargas, a friend of mine, he gets his good looks from his Irish mother and that dark skin from his hand-some Mexican father. He's had my back since we left New Orleans, he is one of us, remember that. Who is the kid with you?'

'Jimmy Treadwell, he rides with me, shared my trou-bles back in Chicago.'

'A botched hold-up and a man dead, for what, $50 if you were lucky? You are not a very good judge of char-acter, Huck, but if you want, he can ride with us. Can he cook?'

'I would have to say he's not the best cook in the world.'

'Well then, it is a good job you did not shoot Emilio there, because he is. The kid can help him.'

Flynn did not want to let the insult go. He took a chance, saying it with a smile but asking outright, 'Is he as good with that gun as he is with his mouth and a skillet?'

'Never learn, will you, Flynn.' It was not a question. 'Show him, Emilio, show the man how you can cook.'

Emilio Vargas smiled the white-toothed smile and drew the steel Colt. The draw was very smooth, the hammer cocked and lowered, spinning the gun on his finger and dropping it back into the leather in one easy motion. The move was so fast it was over before Flynn even realized it had happened. A shudder ran through his big frame.

'I saved your life there, Flynn, that 'breed you insulted is just about the fastest man on the pull I have ever seen, count yourself lucky the rest of your miserable days.' He nodded to Vargas. 'Thanks for not blowing his fool head off, Emilio, we might need him to hold the animals in a couple of days' time, him and the kid both. Flynn is good with horses, that right, Huck?'

'Saved your hide.'

The man called Smitty, a tidy, tall, dapper man in a chequered suit and brown derby hat, poured Flynn a drink and handed it to him, noting the shaking hand and smiled. 'You came close there, mister. Is the kid old enough to drink?'

'Ask him yourself, damn you.' Flynn took his drink to the long bar and sat down. Treadwell shook his head at the offer of a drink and joined him there.

Logan said, 'Smitty, you and Harris put the horses in

the old livery. Flynn's kid can see to it they are fed and watered, then check on friend Flynn's back trail just to be sure and tell Lomax and the boy there to gather some firewood and get some cooking heat out of the stove, I am a hungry man. You up for that, Emilio?'

'Whatever you say, boss. Pronghorn steaks and potatoes best I can do until we get some supplies when we hit Liberty.'

'Liberty?' Flynn got to his feet. 'We going to hit Liberty?'

Logan turned to the big man. 'You know the place?'

'No, but had a run-in with the local law some miles from there – he wore a county badge said he was from Liberty.'

'Know him?'

'Never seen him before. He was an old fool, a nothing kind of man, we can walk right over him.'

'Like you were going to walk right over Vargas.'

Flynn scowled. 'Ask the kid, he will tell you. Took us by surprise when we was trying to help a lady in distress. Knocked me down with his pony and ran us off – stupid bastard gave us back our guns and was we not late to be here, I would have gone back and shot his ass.'

Logan shook his head. 'I can imagine, Huck, I can see you going up against an old man on a horse.' Then picking up his drink he sauntered across the room, light on his feet for a big man, and joined Vargas, picking up the sticky cards, shuffling and dealing a couple of hands of five-card stud. Looking at the cards and tossing them face up on the table, laughing, 'Aces and eights, just isn't my day, old friend.'

Supper over and a few whiskeys later, Ben Logan joined the sad-faced Jimmy Treadwell on the run-down front portico of the Glory Hole. The boy was gazing skywards, watching for a shooting star, hoping it would change his luck which was, to his reckoning, one way or another running pretty low since meeting Huck Flynn.

Squatting beside him on the dusty boards, Logan offered the boy a sack of Bull Durham but the kid shook his head and watched as the outlaw rolled a quirly and fired the dark paper with a blue-topped match. He liked the smell of the fired tobacco but not the raw burn on his throat the one time he had tried it. 'Where did you meet up with Huck?' Logan asked quietly. His voice had a soothing quality to it, easy to listen to; a voice you could trust, maybe even confide in.

'Met him in a bar in Chi soon after I got fired from my job in a general store.'

'Why were you fired?'

'Thieving, the old man said – all I did was eat a candy out of a jar filled with candy and he fired my ass.'

'Huck help you out?'

'Huck said I should get even, knock over the old man's store which we did that very night. Got $6 and two bits for our troubles. Huck said we should do the post office, so we did. The teller pulled an old piece from a safe which misfired and Huck shot him – shot him twice. I told him the second shot was not called for but he said

29

the man had seen us and that was the right thing to do. I heard later the old man did not die, I hope that is true.'

'Not a wise move. Hitting the US Mail Service is federal, they will hunt you down.'

'Was why we lit out, go west young man, bullshit. I don't like it too much out here, especially at night. Are there really wild animals around here will eat you?'

Logan smiled into the darkness. 'Not likely, son, big bears don't come down this low, coyotes howl a lot but keep out of your way, as do the wolves. Might run into a cougar around here and they can kill and feed on a cow but I never heard of one eating a man. No, rattlesnakes are most likely to cause you pain and they will keep out of your way if you keep out of theirs.'

'But Huck says. . . .'

'Take my advice and do not pay too much heed to what old Huck Flynn tells you.' Then, changing the subject, 'This lawman you ran into, did he have a name?'

'Griffin Boone if I heard it right, he told Huck that was who he was to ask for if he was of a mind to.'

'This Boone, did he walk with a limp, have a gimpy right leg?'

'He stayed in the saddle. Do you know him, Mr Logan?'

'Maybe, I don't believe so though the name is familiar.'

Logan stood up, patted the boy on the shoulder, stubbed his smoke out on an upright, said goodnight and went back into the saloon wondering what future

there would be for Jimmy Treadwell in the Badlands of
Wyoming Territory. Then wondering what it held for
any of them.

CHAPTER THREE

ARROWHEAD

Living alone for ten years tends to get a man a little set in his ways and I knew it would take me a while to get used to having a woman and a young kid around the place. Not exactly underfoot, but where I would not expect them to be and I was glad it was only going to be a very temporary arrangement.

After checking on the wagon and at least making an effort to protect their belongings from the elements for whatever time it would take to repair the wheel, it was nearly dark by the time we arrived back at Arrowhead. I got one of the Mexican hands to see to the mare and the two mules and asked Henry Mendoza's wife to check out the spare room for bedding and whatever else a female visitor with a young son might need. Maria, a rotund and good-natured woman took charge of the pair and I bid them goodnight and retired to my office (which was in actual fact a corner of the main living-cum-dining room) and to a glass or two of Hector Thomas' excellent moonshine together with the single daily cheroot I allowed myself. I lit the cigar and opened a window to appease Maria, who otherwise in the morning would chastise me with a lashing tongue telling me that Arrowhead stank like the inside of a whorehouse. I never dared to question her knowledge, but assumed she would have, many times in their lives together, had to drag the rambunctious Henry from such places.

I wondered about the woman and what she may have gone through, being the widow of a Confederate soldier whilst left to live her life and that of the boy on the east coast. I doubted she would have been treated as anyone other than the person she was in Wyoming. The territory had little contact with the Civil War, no battles were fought there and beef from the ranches thereabouts was in all probability consumed by hungry soldiers from both sides, be they wearing the butternut grey or the blue. I looked at the sepia photograph on the side table and at the bunch of flowers Maria always set there beside it, wondering what my visitor would make of that when she saw it.

I was up early the next morning washed, shaved and on my way to Liberty just as the sun was breaking over the distant mountains far to the east of Arrowhead, a sight I never wearied of, a new beginning as every new day is. I had ordered one of the younger hands to take the buckboard out to the stranded wagon, retrieve the wheel, any trunks or cases and bring them back to the ranch to store in the barn for safety, thinking it might well take me more than a couple of days to find a new guide for the Otis woman and her boy on their long journey south. I selected one of the younger hands as I reckoned if one of the older men went along, he would dawdle at Heck Thomas's place and partake of too much 'shine, it being a warm day and a long drive.

Liberty was still half asleep so I had an early breakfast in the Chinaman's Dead Duck Café – an odd name but always a fine breakfast of ham and three eggs over easy. Kang, the old man who owned the café went way back to the beginnings of the Territory and he claimed that one time Bill Cody had eaten a breakfast in the Duck and in honour of the old rascal, he had a framed picture of the buckskin-clad man leaning on a big-bored buffalo gun and smiling for the camera.

After a coffee and a brief chat with my neighbour Will Rider, mostly about the weather and the price of beef, the former being good and the latter not so much, I dropped by the general store, exchanged pleasantries with Mose the storekeeper and purchased a colourful ladies' yellow and red scarf and three sticks of striped peppermint candy. An impulse purchase, after which I made my way down to the courthouse, a large adobe building, home to the county lockup and the sheriff's office. Joe Sawyer greeted me with his usual smile. The happiest man I ever did meet, a boisterous manner which was not at all in keeping with his skeletal-like appearance, his narrow body seemingly held together with a grey wool suit, leather vest and gun rig. I shook hands and handed him the money I had collected, telling him that Heck Thomas would be by later in the month but if he wanted a jug before then he would have to go get it himself.

'Cantankerous old bastard, he had the money there with him I bet but too mean to part with it easy-like. You ever going to buy that two-by-four place, Griff?'

'I have offered but he wants to hang on as long as he can and I appreciate that. He hints it will be mine when the big bear finally comes by and eats him so I guess it will be part of Arrowhead one day, no hurry on my part though.'

'You have $12 due from last month, you want me to send it to the usual charity?'

He smiled, knowing full well what the answer would be. I nodded and said, 'You have any recent flyers might relate to Chicago over the last few months?'

'That's a long ways off, Griff, why the interest?'

'Just a thought, ran into a couple of scarecrows out on my south range, they turned nasty so I had to run them off.' I told him about the broken wagon and the woman and boy staying at Arrowhead. 'I will also be looking for a reliable guide to see them clear of Wyoming and as near to Texas as possible.'

'That man might be hard to find this time of the year but the flyers we can take a looksee at right now.'

He spread several sheets on his desktop, mostly pictures of hard cases that would never see Liberty as a destination; there were only two relating to crimes in Chicago. One was for a gambler who had shot and wounded a faro dealer and the other was for a robbery gone wrong in which a US Mail clerk had been brutally shot and wounded during what the flyer described as 'the felonious act'. The feds were offering a $500 reward for a man named Raymond 'Huck' Flynn. The face on the poster and the man I had felled with the mare were one and the same, of that there was no doubt. There was no mention of the kid who rode with him so perhaps he had not been in any way involved in the robbery. For some reason, I hoped not.

'That's him sure enough, no mention of the kid though.'

'They headed this way?' Suddenly the old man's dark eyes were lighting up; he was old school, a hands-on lawman.

'The woman said she heard them talking about having a good time in Glory.'

'The only lively time they will get there is if maybe they get their asses bit by a rattler. Haven't been by there in years but a ghost town only gets to be more of a ghost town as the years roll by.'

'Maybe I should take a ride out there.'

'It's way out of my jurisdiction, Griff, part of Sioux County. Leave it with me, I will wire Gus Winters and send him the flyer in the mail, tell him what you heard, he can deal with it as he sees fit. You can take a look if it worries you some but it can't be with the county dollar and it is a long ride on a mere possibility. No, I suggest we let Winters deal with it, he is one lazy bastard.'

I thought about that on my ride back to the ranch. It probably was best as it was unlikely that Flynn would take up my invitation and come by Liberty looking for me. He did not strike me as that kind of a man. It was mid-afternoon when the mare and I started on the down slope to the ranch house. The building was white and glistened in the sun. The aspens my wife and I had planted together along the avenue leading to the front of the house whispered a welcome as I fancied they always did and would continue to do long after my passing. The front yard was spotted with a well-watered raised flower bed, a horse trough and an iron pump leading to a well, fed by the creaking windmill above it. Off to one side was the bunkhouse, a small cabin extension, a large red barn and the cook shack. I employed six ranch hands, three of whom were Mexican or of Mexican extraction, and I guessed, kin of Henry Mendoza, the other three were older and had been working the ranch long before I had purchased it at auction and kept them on as the crew. A wise move on my part as they knew the range, the many moods of the weather and how to work cattle with the minimum of fuss. They were loyal to a fault and were almost as devastated as I had been when my wife had passed.

I could see the woman in the yard watering the flowers, the youngster close by, moving when she moved, she ruffled his head and I could imagine she was soothing his fears the way a mother would.

The mare was anxious for water so we pushed on down, the woman looked up and gave me a tired smile of welcome. The boy just stared at me, then moved forward to where the horse had its nose deep into the water, asking me, 'Does he have a name, Sheriff?'

'No son, and he is a she, a mare and I do not believe that she does have a given name, I just call her "horse". I have heard one of the hands call her Daisy but that is a name I do not much care for.'

'Oh, I think Daisy is a nice name, don't you, Chuck?' The woman said quietly, joining us by the well.

The boy looked from me to his mother, not sure which one of us to agree with and wisely for his years, deciding best not to agree either way. He stroked the animal's wet muzzle.

I laughed and his mother smiled, relaxed a little. 'You have some lovely flowers here, did you plant these?'

'No,' I said, 'my wife cared for the flowers and I cared for the grass and the cattle.' Then changing the subject, 'The smith in Liberty will fix the wheel when it is brought in and take it back out with one of my hands and bring the wagon back here. I have arranged to have your trunks brought in for safety, although it's unlikely that they would have been touched – not too many passers-by out by that creek.'

'Thank you, I will of course pay you for your trouble.'

'Finding a guide may not be so easy though, I have put the word out there and that is all I can do.'

'Thank you again, Mr Boone.'

'Call me Griff, most everyone else does and with respect, there is no need to thank me anymore, we help each other out here, it's a way of life. Those two you met on the trail were from Chicago, the older man is wanted for armed robbery there. If he is in Glory the sheriff of that county will be informed so it is no longer our problem. Have you eaten yet?'

'Maria fixed us breakfast and we had sandwiches for lunch, we have been well cared for.'

The boy was still petting the mare and she seemed to

38

approve. On impulse I walked over, picked him up and swung him on to the saddle. He looked down at me, surprised and trembling, I sensed his mother moving forward protectively as a mother bear or a she-wolf might. I did not hesitate. 'Pick up the reins, Chuck, she likes you up there I can tell, we can walk her over to the stable, feed her, give her a rub down, would you like that?' Suddenly the trembling ceased and he leaned down and took up the reins as I held the hackamore, touched my hat to his mother and led him toward the stable. He looked back once at his mother and broke into a smile, lighting up the whole front yard of Arrowhead.

'That was a nice thing you did with Chuck and your horse, I think in some way it made up for the bad of the past few weeks.'

'I should have asked your permission first though, sorry about that, but I am given to acting on impulse.'

'It was intuition, you knew he wanted more of the animal and you gave it him and that deserves another thank you, I am afraid.'

Laura Otis was relaxed, sipping a glass of red wine, sitting on the leather chair in front of the cold fire, being stared down upon by a large painting of the Seventh Cavalry and the whole Sioux nation fighting an imagined battle somewhere out on a barren prairie. We shared the supper Maria had prepared, much to her husband's dismay at being kicked out of the kitchen and sent back to his duties in the cook shack.

'Would you mind if I smoked?' I asked.

'Of course not, it's your house and anyway I rather like the smell of tobacco – although I would never touch it myself.'

'Did your husband smoke?'

'Sometimes, a pipe and black tobacco, it was a dreadful smell, clung to the curtains.'

I fired the cheroot, enjoying the rush of the inhaled smoke, wondering if she was going to tell me more but instead she asked a question of her own, her eyes returning to the photograph as they had so many times during supper. 'Your wife was beautiful.'

'I cannot argue with you there.'

'What was her given name?'

'Martha Jane Riordan.'

She studied the photograph at some length before speaking again. It was a sepia photograph taken in West Texas, a handsome woman seated, a tall man standing at her side. The woman wore a white floral-patterned dress which flowed around the wooden chair. She was smiling. The tall bearded man at her side was dressed in the uniform of an officer of the Army of Northern Virginia, the Confederate butternut grey, he had a captain's insignia on the jacket, yellow piped grey pants and tall black leather boots. I knew what she wanted to ask but was fascinated to see if she would. She chose not to pry so I gave an answer of sorts to the unasked question. 'We met before the war, I joined the army soon after Fort Sumner. I was a Texan – what else was I to do.' It was not a question.

'I was not prying, sir, please forgive my rudeness.'

'I was attached to General John Bell Hood's Texas

Brigade, soldiered with him from Bull Run, Gettysburg through to Chickamauga, never got a scratch – not even at Little Round Top. Then, near the end of the war at Nashville, I had my horse shot from under me by a Union sharpshooter and three Minie balls in my right leg and hip. I saw out the rest of the conflict in a field hospital. The leg was saved by a competent young surgeon, who told me through gritted teeth that he had amputated enough legs that day and he would save mine even if he had to tie it on with bailing wire and fishing line. That leg still troubles me in the cold of winter but now, in spring and summer, I hardly limp.'

She was silent, listening to a story I rarely told.

'At the end of the war with the money I had saved and earned the hard way, Martha and I moved north. Texas was not a good place to be during reconstruction, nowhere in the south was. I bought Arrowhead at auction for a song, and here I still am. There is no north and south in this part of the country, it was not really part of the war and the folk hereabouts could not care less whether or not I wore the Blue or the Grey. Your business is not my business, ma'am, but you should maybe think on that before heading off for Texas. Wild horses, and we have plenty of them, would not drag me from here.'

I did not know why I felt compelled to tell her my story, but somehow I did and was a little embarrassed by the outpouring. I coughed, got to my feet and refilled my glass, surprised at her acceptance of more wine. I went to the table and reached into my saddlebags, dumped there as usual when I entered the house, lazily awaiting Maria to hang them on one of the antler hooks by the door, glaring at me if I was around. I handed her the scarf and the candy. 'The candy is for Chuck, the scarf for you – you need all the protection you can in this sun, especially on the back of your neck. I have asked Henry to scare up a hat for Chuck, I wouldn't know what size hat he could wear and still see where he was going.'

She smiled, the first real smile on her sad face I had seen. It lightened up the room much as the boy's had lit up the yard. 'Thank you, it is very kind of you, both to Charlie and myself.'

'You are both welcome and now, if you will excuse me, I have to go over some ranch chores with my top hand. Sleep well.'

'And you also, Griff, goodnight.'

I watched her leave the room, a graceful woman and I liked the way she said my name, liked it very much.

CHAPTER FOUR

SIOUX FALLS

Sioux County sheriff Gus Winters never did care for Monday mornings; they were always overloaded with the week ahead, laying it out for him, pushing him in directions he did not always want to travel and he did not think this Monday morning would be any different to those many Monday mornings that had gone before. In short, he was not in the best of moods. He pushed open his office door and dumped the sheaf of papers he had carried from the post office on to his already cluttered desk. Gus Winters was not a tidy man in any respect other than his mode of dress. He wore black wool pants, vest, tie and, when cool enough, a long black frock coat. He was a big man, clean shaven, his face coloured by years of Wyoming weather, sun blasted in the summer and snow chilled in the winter. He was a lawman first and foremost but being a politician was a close run second. He was ambitious and old enough, and some considered wise enough, to be listened to. The clothing was window dressing. It made him, he believed, look like a lawman. Twice elected sheriff of Sioux County, he expected to take a step up and run for mayor come the next election. Mayor of Sioux Falls, the county seat, sounded good to him. He was no longer a young man and smart dressing helped with the image. At forty-eight he was a little young for mayor but a little old for sheriff of such a large county and he knew the move upwards would have to come now.

Leaving the door open to let in some fresh morning air to kill the stink of yesterday's tobacco smoke, he lit the stove and placed the coffee pot on top, opened up the shutters and disturbed a blow fly which buzzed noisily around the room before settling back on the window. Rolling up an old copy of the County News, he slapped the fly, spreading a little white blood-speckled greasy mark across the glass. Something for one of the deputies (he had three of them although one was only part-time) to clean up later in the day. He dumped the newspaper in the waste basket and settling his big frame down behind the desk, he set a pair of wire-framed glasses on his hooked nose. First he examined the scribbled telegraphs before opening the mail; it was his routine, as were most of the telegrams. One stood out from the rest, a wire from Joe Sawyer, the elderly sheriff of the neighbouring Liberty County. He read it once and he then read it again; it was a lot to think about, an opportunity perhaps to help with that leg up the political ladder. It read simply: RAYMOND 'HUCK' FLYNN WANTED FOR ATTEMPTED MURDER AND ROBBERY OF CHICAGO

POST OFFICE, REWARD OF $500 OFFERED BY FEDERAL AUTHOR-
ITIES. MAY BE IN COMPANY OF AT LEAST ONE OTHER MAN.
RELIABLE INFORMATION IS HE MAY BE HEADED FOR GLORY.
ARMED AND DANGEROUS, POSTER TO FOLLOW TOMORROW
NOON STAGE. I URGE CAUTION. Regards JOE SAWYER,
LIBERTY COUNTY.

Winters read the wire again, thinking to himself there
were two big opportunities therein. One, $500 was very
nearly a year's pay and secondly, the capture of such a
fugitive would not only make for good headlines locally
but would also invite some regard from the federal
authorities. Two opportunities not to be disregarded in
an election year. He had time to think it through, drinking strong coffee and awaiting the arrival of the
Wednesday noon stage, which passed through Sioux
Falls on its long journey across Wyoming Territory to
Laramie.

The Liberty County sheriff was as good as his word
and on Wednesday morning, the reward poster with its
monochrome likeness of the fugitive Huck Flynn lay on
his desk along with the much-read telegraph. All he had
to do was measure up the risk, evaluate the gain in
bringing the outlaw in and how best to go about it to
ensure a successful venture. Winters was a lawman; a
tough lawman, age and inaction had perhaps slowed his
reflexes and he had no real desire to sit a horse for the
long hard ride to Glory but, politics aside, he did take
his oath to the folk of Sioux County very seriously.
Thing was to ensure success with the slightest of risks
and minimum of discomfort. He had two reliable full-
time deputies in Mort Howard and Jim Serino, both

capable men, handy with fist or gun and men who would trust and follow him. The walls of the office suddenly seemed to close in around him and he felt the urge to be in an open space, room to breathe; a ride to Glory would be just the thing and quite suddenly he was filled with a sense of purpose far and above his own personal ambitions. The lawman was kicking in with the politician taking to the shady grey of the background.

The ever-present Wyoming wind, cooling in summer and bitterly cold in winter, increased steadily as the long duster-clad trio of lawmen made their way across the rock-strewn scrub and gazed down upon the ruin that once was Glory. He had thought about it long and hard before deciding on taking the two full-time deputies with him, leaving J.C. Baldwin, the part-time deputy and one-time county sheriff, in charge during what he hoped would be a brief absence. They had packed provisions and gear for an overnight stay should it prove necessary but, again, he hoped not.

'Damned place always did give me the creeps, it just up and died over two days, one day seeming to thrive and the next empty when some asshole discovered gold up by Shelby Creek which, as it often happened, turned out to be worthless fool's gold and so they just moved on. Why they did not come back I have no idea, I guess it was just played out and any excuse to move on was good enough.' There was a wistfulness in his tone. Winters had originally come west in search of gold himself but that was in the Dakotas and he arrived far too late, something he promised himself would never happen again.

'I see two horses outside what could have been a saloon, looks to be the Glory Hole, but nothing more,' said Howard, the younger of the two deputies. He lowered his field glasses and asked, 'We go right on down or leave one of us up here, how do you want to play it, Sheriff?'

'We will ride down together but you hold back with the horses when we go in, wouldn't want to be afoot this far from home.' He smiled and pushed the pinto he was riding down the rocky trail, taken only a few days earlier by Flynn and Treadwell.

They dismounted in silence, Winters and Serino tying off their ponies at the hitching rail, their mounts greeted with a tired interest by the two animals already there. He did not recognize the brands so he guessed they were from out of county.

Howard stayed mounted.

Winters led the way, pushing through the creaking, broken batwing doors and into the dusty gloom of what was once the social hub of Glory. There were two men in the room, one a dark-skinned Mexican and the other a tall man dressed in black, a man who could easily have been mistaken for a lawman himself. The Mexican smiled, his teeth flashing in the gloom, a wide smile of greeting. The tall man nodded, stepped forward. 'Welcome to Glory, gents, we can offer you a drink of 'shine or spring water but vittles have we none.' He smiled the words, 'Ben Logan, just passing through.' He offered his hand and Winters took it, a firm handshake.

'Gus Winters and this here is Jim Serino.' He looked

47

over at the bar to where the Mexican was filling two glass jars with a dark amber liquid.

'Forgive me, this is my partner Emilio Vargas, he fancies himself as a barkeep.'

Winters undid his long coat and the hazy sunlight filtering through the dusty windows caught the polished star on his vest, sending a little beam dancing across the room as he moved forward to the bar, picked up the drink and tossed it back, sucking his teeth at the sudden bite of the alcohol. 'Local 'shine, a booming business around these parts just so long as the marshals keep a blind eye turned to the enterprise.'

'A lawman, sir, an ambition I once had for my own self but turned to cattle buying instead. Not so dangerous and much more profitable. You on the hunt or just out for a ride?' A hint of sarcasm in the Irish lilt.

'I don't know anyone who rides for pleasure in this wind and as far as cattle buying goes, in this county it is only a safe enterprise just so long as the cattle you are buying actually belong to the man you are buying them from.' Winters smiled back at the big man, finding out about each other without intruding or seeming overly curious.

Serino stepped forward, careful not to walk between the two men and taking his jar, smiled at the Mexican who refilled his own and raised it to the deputy. 'Salud.'

'I am looking for a man,' Winters said, 'he may have passed through here a day or so ago, name's Huck Flynn, big man, near as big as you, big nose. Have you seen such a man here in Glory?'

'No, sir, but we only got here last night, resting our

horses before riding on for Liberty. I have a cattle deal going down there.'

'Your animals are not getting a lot of rest tied off to a hitching rail all night.'

'Gave them a little exercise this morning, tried to find them something to eat that wasn't sage of which there is plenty. Had to cut it short though due to the wind. We'll be moving on directly.'

Winters did not like the way it was shaping up, the man was too confident. There were no beeves to buy in Liberty, the roundup was long over and the cattle long gone to Abilene. 'I guess we will be on our way then,' he nodded to Serino, 'Water the horses, Jim, and tell Mort we are moving along.'

'Three of you?' It was the Mexican. 'There are three of you? Why not ask your friend in for a drink?'

'He's a member of the Church, part-time preacher, never touches the stuff.' The words were almost drowned by a rapid burst of gunfire and a scream from out on the street.

Huck Flynn watched as the riders scrambled down the rocky trail and reined in outside of the Glory Hole. Two of the men dismounted and entered the saloon but the third simply walked his horse to the rail and sat there, watching. After a while Treadwell asked, 'They look like law to you, Huck?'

'They stink of it, kid, you wait here.' Flynn stepped clear of the broken-down stable door and made his way across the street to where Mort Howard leaned on the pommel of his saddle, trying to hear the conversation from within the saloon. Sensing Flynn's approach, he straightened and turned; one look was enough to recognize the large, unshaven man as the felon from the Liberty flyer that all three men had studied carefully before setting out. He reached for his Colt but was far too late. Flynn shot him out of the saddle and as he tried to rise, Treadwell stepped out of the gloom and shot the downed man twice more. The saddle horse screamed and bolted down the rutted street, closely followed by the other two mounts, one dragging part of the rail. Only the original two mounts remained and stayed firmly tied to what was left of the rail.

Inside the Glory Hole, Gus Winters pulled his gun but was no match for the Mexican who shot him twice, then spinning and shooting Serino in the head, throwing the man sideways and down on top of the fallen Winters. The sheriff was stunned, the bullets raked his left side and one entered his chest but there was no real pain, just a throb, more like a punch from a hard fist than hot lead burning through flesh. He slowly lapsed into a dark place with the roar of the gunshots numbing his ears and the stink of the black powder smoke filling his lungs.

'Goddamn it all to hell,' Logan swore as the grinning Flynn walked into the room, his smoking gun still in his hand. 'Who started the goddamned shooting?'

'John Law outside, he recognized me, pulled his piece.'

'I should have sent you north with Smitty and the others, you are an asshole, what the hell were you doing on the street? I told you to lay low if we had visitors.'

'To hell with you, Ben, I don't take orders as to where I can or cannot go.' As he spoke he raised the muzzle of his Colt but froze there as Vargas whispered, 'I would not do that, señor, I would not do that very much.'

Logan would not let it go. 'How the hell did they know to look for you here?'

'Beats me, maybe that bitch heard us talking.'

'What bitch?'

'The one with the broke-down wagon we told you about.'

'Jesus, there could be a whole posse on the way here, maybe even more out there now.' He turned to Vargas. 'We all packed, Emilio?'

'And ready to ride, Ben,' Vargas said, still keeping his eyes on Flynn. 'That is unless Mr Flynn here has more to say.'

Flynn holstered his gun and walked back into the windy daylight to where Treadwell was staring down at the dead Mort Howard. 'I don't know why I did that, it was just . . .' His voice tailed off as Flynn brushed past him.

'Forget it, kid, mount up, we are riding out of here right now.'

Ben Logan and Emilio Vargas followed him and within three minutes, the men were clear of Glory and headed for the line shack situated four miles to the north of Liberty.

Gus Winters pushed the body of the dead deputy clear and tried to get to his feet but could not make it. He could hear a horse fidgeting at the rail, snorting at the metallic smell of his blood-soaked rider crumpled half on and half off of the rotted boardwalk. He looked out from under the broken batwings; the other two horses were gone. He guessed they were with the outlaws and headed as far and away as possible. He figured he had been hit twice, one bullet in the chest and the other in his side, the latter he could tell from his blood-soaked back had passed straight through. There was no way he could walk, let alone mount a horse and ride, shot up as he was, but to just lie down and die was not an option. He crawled to the bar, pulled himself to his feet and using the roughhewn pine top as a rail he made his way to the rear, where he found the remains of the jug and some dusty bar towels. Cleaning his wounds as best he could with the moonshine and drinking the spring water he had been offered earlier, he settled on one of the barroom chairs, the throbbing and the whiskey inducing a deep and pain-relieving sleep. Sitting there snoring, leaning to the left, his long body draped over the chair's armrests was where Griffin Boone found him seven hours later.

CHAPTER FIVE

GOING TO TEXAS

The Liberty County sheriff Joe Sawyer had a bad cold and a bad case of irritability. He snapped, snuffled and snorted and in general made life difficult for all around him, including me. He was a proud, unambitious man, surprised to have been elected to the office of county sheriff and unlike his old friend Gus Winters, he harboured not a single ambitious inclination to go further in politics. Fed up with his moaning and groaning about everyone and everything I told him to go home and get well and that I would hold the fort until such a time as he could get back to work without upsetting everyone in the county. I was surprised when he took me up on the offer.

'Sure you're OK with this, Griff? I know you have that woman and kid to take care of and need to run Arrowhead but I am a mean sonofabitch when I have a cold.'

'More than OK, Joe, you are a mean sonofabitch when you haven't got one. In point of fact though it suits me greatly.'

He raised an eyebrow and I could see that he wanted to push me on that remark, but he let it slide. His wife, Belle, a long-suffering handsome woman, collected him from the office and taking his arm, led him out into the street giving me a knowing nod and a grateful smile. 'Come by and see me, Griff,' said Joe. 'Make sure young Ross knows what he's doing and keep me informed, will you?'

'Sure I will,' I lied, waving him out.

In a way I really was pleased to have the office to myself; life with my two visitors was not unpleasant on the few times we encountered each other but I was beginning to feel a little awkward around Laura Otis. Mostly I ate in town but we did share a few meals and breakfast was generally a shared affair, with me trying to think of things to say and her pretending to listen to them. The wagon was repaired and sitting in the barn ready for the long haul to Texas if she was still in a mind to go, although we never talked of it and I asked Henry Mendoza to keep the barn doors shut so as she would not be reminded that she was only a visitor to Arrowhead and not a permanent fixture there. I had explained to her that it was getting hard to find her a guide and, to be honest with myself at least, that I had not actually tried very hard to find one anyway.

There was little for me to do in Liberty. I did the rounds, swapped stories with Lassiter, the owner of the small billiard hall which tended to attract gatherings of the town's bored menfolk, checked the incoming mail and posted the wanted poster for Huck Flynn to Gus Winters over in Sioux Falls, just catching the noon Overland. It would take a full day by coach, a journey that would only take a half day or less on a good saddle horse. A horse could go in pretty much a straight line in the wide Wyoming open spaces whereas the Overland followed a twisting well-worn trail, probably first broken by a wandering buffalo and then by every other animal including man until a visible trail was forged. I sought out Jack Ross, the full-time deputy, an inexperienced but willing young man, a bulky man, handy to have close by come roundup time when the drovers hit Liberty or, as was more often the case, on any given payday Saturday night. I told him Gus had gone home sick and I was about to call it a day, so it was his watch.

It was around midday when the mare and I arrived back at Arrowhead, the horse to a buck, a gallop and a dusty roll in the paddock and me to a real cup of joe. Thunder rolled around the foothills but there was no smell of rain on the ever present breeze. I had coffee with Maria Mendoza who informed me that Henry and young Charlie, she refused to call him Chuck, had gone off fishing for bass in one of the many tributaries of the Liberty River which traversed my property. I crossed the yard and asked one of the crew sitting around having a midday smoke and a short break from fence-mending on the lower ranges to hitch a team to the buggy – it felt like a good afternoon for a ride. Back in the house, I gathered together a slicker, should it chance to rain, and a couple of apples from the bowl Maria kept replenished, insisting I did not eat enough fruit, a canteen of fresh water, a small jug of Hector's moonshine, my twelve gauge should I run into a brace of duck and headed out the front door and on to the veranda.

Laura Otis was standing there, gazing out across the paddock towards the stand of cottonwoods and the open countryside beyond. I wondered if she had visited the shaded stand of trees and seen Martha's grave with its stone marker and iron railed fence, and noticed how carefully tended it was with a constantly refreshed bowl of flowers. I hoped she had.

I stopped by the door and on impulse, a trait I am generally noted for, said quietly, 'Lovely day for a ride out, would you care to join me?' She looked at me long and hard, wondering I guess did I genuinely want her company or was I just being polite to a guest? 'Come on, it would be good for you, get yourself a slicker off the hook just in case of rain, you can share my canteen,' and added, smiling reassuringly I hoped, 'you can pack your own apples though.'

'I would love to if you are sure it is not too much trouble.' Always that polite response to anything I ever offered her or did for the boy. Then waiting for the reassurance she hoped would come. I wondered just what sort of a rough time she had experienced in the long years since her husband's death.

'I would enjoy your company very much.'

She almost ran into the house and while she was gone, I walked to where Maria was tending her chickens and told her we were going for a ride and may be back late, so could she put the boy to bed and reassure him all was well.

'Going for a ride, coming back late, Mr Griffin?' She beamed knowingly and I shook my head in despair.

Laura was back within minutes carrying a yellow slicker, a bulky paper bag and two apples; smiling happily she made for the buggy and I helped her up, offering her the traces but she politely declined and leaned back on the padded seat. We drove for an hour due south towards the county line, which bordered both Liberty and Sioux Falls. We paused only once, for Laura to paddle in a pebbled clear water stream from which I had flushed a pair of ducks, dropping them both with one barrel of the twelve gauge. I dumped the birds in the boot of the buggy. 'Supper, one each, build a fire later on the way back, cook them, eat them, pioneer style.' It made her laugh. It was a pleasant, gentle sound, a genuine laugh, a whisper in the wind. A sad moment, it so reminded me of Martha.

We did as I had promised and late afternoon, after showing her the warm springs on my property, we were back at the creek where I made a ring of stones, built a small but hot campfire, plucked the birds, cut two forked cottonwood sticks and with the birds spitted on a third stick, sat back and watched them roast, the fat from the plump birds dripping and sizzling on the hot coals. Laura produced the bag which, back at the house, she had thoughtfully filled with fresh bread and cheese and a couple of hard-boiled eggs left over from her salad supper the previous evening, and I took out the jug of moonshine and offered her the first sip. She did not decline which both surprised and pleased me. We sat like that on a blanket, the silence broken only by the croaking of a bullfrog out looking for a mate, but taking care not to expose himself to the hoot owl that had also made us aware of his presence.

'Is this a place you visit frequently?' she asked, her voice low, not wanting to make too big a hole in the natural silence of the evening. 'With a frog and an owl?'

'Which am I?' I asked, a silly question but the alcohol was affecting my thinking.

'Which indeed?'

I did not answer but posed a question of my own. 'What was your husband's name?' I waited for the long silence to pass.

'Charles, Charlie Otis, I named the boy after him. He never saw his son, but it is something for Charlie to remember and think on when he is old enough.'

'Infantry, cavalry?' I pressed on.

She sighed, a deep sigh as if relieved to be talking a little about her life, sharing maybe as I had shared mine. 'Neither, he was not a warrior, he never carried or fired a gun in his life. He was a gentle man, a doctor, a surgeon. He was killed, they told me, by cannon fire just outside of Richmond in the last days of the war.'

'Hard times,' I said, passing her the jug and watching as she took a small swallow before handing it back to me.

'Very hard, Griff, but tell me why is it harder to be killed at the very end of a war rather than at the beginning of one? The first soldier killed in combat is just as dead either way, so is it because if you serve almost to the very end you feel that you have earned the right to hope for survival?'

I had often wondered that myself and never found a reasonable answer. Perhaps that was because there isn't one, there is never any explanation for a war, any war, in which some men live and some men die. It is the very nature of war, someone starts it and someone finishes it and in between many men who had nothing to do with either the beginning or the end die. I got to my feet, stifling the groan as my right leg reminded me of how close I myself had come to not making it through to Appomattox Court House. 'It's getting late, I guess we should head back to home, Chuck may be wondering what I have done with his mother.'

She got to her feet, more gracefully than I and said, 'Pass me the jug, cowboy, one last swig to a peaceful night for us and Mr Bullfrog. You go first, sir.'

I took a long swig and passed her the jug before agreeing that she take care of the fire while I fetched the buggy I had left in the shade of the cottonwoods. The horses were pleased to see me and I gave them a couple of handfuls of pony nuts before tightening the tack. I took a quick leak behind one of the cottonwood trees, leaving enough time for her should her needs be the same as mine, before leading the pair back to the creek for a drink. She was an outdoor lady, of that there was no doubt. The campsite was squared away, soil mixed with gravel from the creek bed on the dead fire ready for the next wayfarer passing by.

Wyoming Territory was and probably always would be full of sky and in the night-time it was even more so. There was no moon to speak of but the dark sky

was littered with bright, twinkling stars that gave generously of their light and lit the prairie grass through
which we drove with an eerie silver sheen. I think she
was a little lightheaded from the moonshine and
happily burbled on about the stars, pointing out the
constellations to me one after the other. I saw them as
clusters and could never quite see the shapes of
hunters, crabs, bears or fish that appeared so easily
familiar to others and I told her so, then chuckling as
a childhood thought crossed my mind. '*Moon light,
starlight, the boogieman will not be out tonight.*'

'What are you laughing at, me going on about stars?'

'No, really I am not, just a childhood memory.'

'Ah, sometimes they are the best of memories but
seemingly always the most elusive.'

I changed the subject. 'The only star I know for sure
is the North Star.'

She laughed, a sound I was beginning to look forward
to. 'The Pole Star, the star every cowboy and sailor can
find.'

'Did you know a lot of sailors?' I asked, my tongue
firmly in my cheek.

'No, Mr Boone, I did not know many sailors. Only the
one, only Charlie Otis, he was a sailor before he joined
the army. A sailor in the army, who can figure things like
that?'

'Sorry,' I said, 'I did not know that.'

'No need to be sorry, how could you have done.' It
wasn't a question and she touched my arm briefly in
some hidden acknowledgement that she had not taken
offence at my remark.

We finished the last mile in silence and I wondered if she was asleep. She wasn't, saying 'Home at last, kind sir,' as we pulled into the front yard to be met immediately by Mendoza, who took the reins after helping Laura down from the rig.

Her first question, as I suspected it would be, was as to the welfare of the boy. Mendoza laughed, his teeth flashing in the light from the oil lamp burning brightly by the large front door of Arrowhead. 'He is asleep and we are all going to be eating crappies for the foreseeable future, that boy can really fish.'

And that is how the evening ended for Laura Otis as she thanked me, touched my arm again and walked through to the guest bedroom, closing the door quietly behind her.

The evening was not over for me though and I took a jug and a glass from the side table and settled with them on one of the veranda rockers. Suddenly I was feeling very lonely, not alone but lonely, wondering at the subtle difference between the two words, then as if in answer to my wandering thoughts Henry Mendoza joined me, sitting on the other chair, nodding his head. The elderly man did not speak but handed me his sack of makings and in return I handed him my jug. We sat there like that, two old friends, long into the early morning.

The morning following our evening picnic I was sitting in the office reading a wire from Gus Winters, thanking me for the flyer which had arrived as promised and informing me that he was considering taking a couple

61

of deputies to check on the Glory situation. I wired back advising extreme caution. I was still sitting there thinking about it when Laura Otis tapped on the door and asked me if I was busy. I said no and offered her a coffee, at which she took one look and wisely declined.

'Problem?' I asked, noting the concern on her face and the heightened colour of her cheeks. After she was seated in front of my desk I moved around to sit close to her and perched my left buttock on its corner, not wanting to intimidate her in any way as so often can be the case when one person has to face another across a desk. Three feet can seem like a mile.

'Not really a problem, I just need someone I can trust to talk to,' she said.

'Then I am happy that you thought of me,' I said, and meaning it.

'It's just that I have been thinking about what you said the other day, about going to Texas. Do you recall the conversation?'

'Of course,' I said, 'was I out of line on that?'

'No, silly, it is simply that it took a while to sink in, so much has happened to me in the last few years that sometimes it seems best to simply sit back and ponder, another way of doing nothing.' The hint of a smile.

'We have all been to that place, Laura, some of us many times.'

'I find that hard to believe in your case, Griff.'

'Believe it,' I said.

She studied her hands for a moment, the long slender fingers curling and straightening in rapid succession, then seeming to have made a decision she said,

62

'You are right, it is a long way and would probably put us in danger for no real purpose. In other words I think I might take your advice.' She paused looking at me expecting me to ask or reassure her either way. I said nothing. 'I have met some very nice people here, Tildy the schoolteacher tells me she needs help – I do have some experience in the teaching field and also the storekeeper told me he could use a woman's help dealing with the millinery side of his business, especially on paydays. So you see, I could fend for myself and Charlie.'

I got up and poured a cup of the thick black joe that Ross had started on the boil that morning, and spooned in some sugar. 'And. . . ?' I asked, to break the silence.

'And I can sell the wagon, pay you what I owe you and I have enough money in the bank to rent or maybe even buy a small house in town, somewhere for the boy and I to call home.'

'You don't owe me anything,' I said, 'helping each other is what we do around here. You don't have to rush away from Arrowhead either, you are more than welcome to stay just as long as you like.' Then adding softly, 'I like having you both there.'

'Here or there, do you think it is a good idea, my staying I mean?'

'I think it's a great idea. I don't believe you will regret it, in a couple of years or maybe less Wyoming Territory will become a state and that will be one proud day. Tell you what, let's go over to the Dead Duck Café and I'll buy you lunch and a decent cup of coffee by way of a cel-ebration.' I felt like celebrating and hoped that my

63

enthusiasm for her decision to stay in Liberty County did not trouble her.

'I would like that very much, Griff.' Then asking, 'Do you ever take that hat off? I don't think I have ever seen you without it, not even indoors.'

'It is a very fine hat, Laura, a Stetson, Boss of the Plains, beaver felt, cost me $20 in Cheyenne, I intend to get my full money's worth out of it.'

'Well, sir, that told me.'

She took my arm as we walked down Main Street and across to the Chinaman's place, I touched the brim of my hat to Joe Sawyer's wife as she came out of the post office, she smiled happily at me and I knew she could not then wait to get home and tell her husband that she had seen me with a lady on my arm, not something anyone in Liberty had seen for going on ten years.

Lawmen are not made, they are born; a badge, an election or an appointment cannot fashion a good lawman. It had never been my intention to get behind a badge even part-time and even though I was asked to stand for county sheriff once, I declined. I enjoyed ranching, working with my men, the quiet life of a rancher. The Indians gave our part of the country very little trouble, unlike up on the Big Horn range where a certain blond-haired general had come amiss at the hands of the united forces of the Northern Cheyenne, Arapaho and the Sioux. The trouble that followed stayed in the north and allowed us get on with the raising of the hundreds of beef cattle needed to feed the growing population, the almost insatiable hunger of an expanding nation.

The range wars, large or small, born out of greed did not touch us down in Liberty. Even so, we still needed law and order and while men like Joe Sawyer and Gus Winters held the political ground, men such as myself, Wyatt Earp in Arizona (a high profile lawman), Wes Harper, Frank Tombs and John Dancer, US marshal Harry Boudine, and others pursued the calling in their own quiet way. And, in my own quiet way my gut told me that Gus Winters was a fool to head for Glory with just two deputies. Huck Flynn was not Glory-bound on a whim, it was something much bigger driving him on. I worried about these things all afternoon and even over a supper shared with Laura Otis and her young son I could not shake the feeling of foreboding that entrenched itself in some dark place within me.

After supper, Charlie in bed and the dishes cleared, my help having been refused, Laura joined me on the veranda, sitting in the rocking chair beside me, sharing a bottle of wine bought for the occasion in Liberty that afternoon. I fired my cheroot and blew the smoke in a ring, watching as it collapsed at the sides and spread out, finally vanishing in the warm breeze drifting across the long grass to the south of Arrowhead.

'What troubles you tonight, Griff? You have been so quiet. Nothing to do with my deciding on making a home here, I hope.'

'Of course not, I told you I am delighted you have decided on Liberty, Texas would have been a long way to travel for a visit.'

'You would have visited us in Texas?'

'There is a saying here in the west, when someone

wants to vanish, that they have gone to Texas. It is big and although a man can get lost there forever that does not mean he has really gone to Texas – just that he has disappeared. I wouldn't want you to disappear and I believe you know that.'

She did not answer right away, thinking on those words and finally saying, 'That is so nice to hear but as a friend, and I feel we are friends, I need you to share with me. It has been a long time since I shared any deep thoughts with another and it is difficult for me to suddenly want to know, deeply know, another person and I don't like it that you are so troubled.'

'The men who gave you grief when your wagon was crippled are, or at least one of them is, wanted for robbery and attempted murder in Chicago. You told me you had heard them mention Glory – well, Glory is nothing more than a ghost town, an old deserted mining camp in the low land just below our border with Sioux County to the south of here. We were close to that county line when we were by the creek yesterday. I wired the sheriff there and he has taken it upon himself to lead a couple of deputies into Glory and see if Flynn is there.' I paused, giving it some thought, sipping my wine and listening to the crickets as if they could tell me what was going down in the rocky foothills beyond the long, yellow grass of Liberty.

'Thing is, I cannot see Flynn travelling from Chicago just to ride into a run-down mining camp. I have a feeling, and it is only a feeling, that there is a bigger game afoot and the damned fool sheriff may run afoul of it. Worse, it was my word that sent him there.'

CHAPTER SIX

A TOWN CALLED GLORY

Long after Laura had gone to bed, I still studied on the problem and the discomfort I felt at having put Winters on the trail of Huck Flynn and finally decided that, come first light, I would head out to Glory and join forces with him and his deputies. And that is exactly what I did. Packing a few supplies and the office medical kit into my saddle bags I headed the mare out across the grassland, towards the county line and a town called Glory.

I approached the ghost town from the high north which I felt would give a better perspective than that of the lower, more familiar trail and resting the mare on the crest of a narrow defile, the rough trail leading down into Glory, I swept the main street and the dilapidated building with my army field glasses. There was a man down half on and half off the broken boardwalk outside of what appeared to be a saloon and the only really serviceable building on the street. There was no sign of smoke issuing from the steel chimney which ran up the side of the building. A dozen or so crows were gathered on the man's upper torso, doing what carrion crows do best. There was a lone saddle horse wandering along the street, snuffling at the sage that had sprung up after the departure of the miners who had once lived there, be it for only a brief year if the stories were true. The animal's saddle had twisted and hung from beneath its belly, the stirrups dragging along the dusty ground. The hitching rail was broken. I watched for thirty minutes or so and then, certain that I was alone, I pushed the mare down through the rocks and walked her slowly along the rutted street. The loose horse saw us and walked to meet us, greeting the mare as a long-lost friend, snorting and bumping against my leg. I could see that the saddle and the back of the horse were caked in dried blood. I reined in, dismounted and carefully stripped the displaced saddle, checking to see if the animal was wounded in any way. Satisfied that the blood was from another source I took my carbine from the saddle boot, worked the lever and lowered the hammer to half cock, the only safety the weapon offered. The crows scattered as I approached the saloon, the faded banner of which read Glory Hole Saloon, and stepped over the dead man. His eyes were gone and with them most of the soft tissue of the eye sockets and cheeks, his bones clearly visible. I supposed he had been dead at least twelve hours and probably more; there was a bloody Sioux County deputy's badge pinned to his red shirt and an undrawn revolver on his hip.

With my rifle pointing forward, I used the barrel to push open the broken batwing and stepped inside.

It was a mess: the metallic stink of battlefield blood, the floor covered with it, dried and caked beneath the body of another man, a star plainly visible on his vest and a bullet wound to his head just below the hairline and pretty much dead centre.

I heard a low moan and for the first time, noticed the sagging body of a man half on and half off a barroom chair, his back was turned toward me but it was unmistakeably the narrow shoulders of Gus Winters. I knelt down beside him. 'Can you hear me. Gus? It's me, Griffin Boone.' He fixed me with half closed eyes, the hint of a smile. His shirt was covered in blood, mostly dried blood. He did not speak or offer any sound as I examined his chest and side. The chest wound was the worst but had bled the least. Most of the blood was from a wound in his side and had leaked through the dirty cloth he had somehow fixed by jamming the ends into his pants top. It was a through and through and if he was lucky and the round had not hit anything vital, would heal. The chest wound was different, the bullet was still buried in there somewhere and way beyond my limited medical skill. I fetched my saddle bags and took out the kit carried by most ranch hands that lived, worked and died a long ways from a settlement or regular medical help. I cleaned the wounds and bandaged them as best I could and waited.

'Hurts like hell, Griff . . . You alone?' His voice was

weak but clear.

'Yes, I came alone.'

'He was here, your man Flynn, three or four others, shot us all to hell. Mort and Serino, you seen them?'

'Sorry, Gus, they're both dead and I have to get you out of here or you soon will be. Does the Dutchman still run that little two-by-four outfit south of here?'

He nodded.

'OK, you hang tight, take a swig of this if it gets to hurting too bad – it's laudanum so go easy. I'm going to catch up the loose horse, one of yours I think. I'll get you aboard and leave you with the Hagers while I head for Sioux Falls and a doctor, I don't think you can travel that far.'

'Whatever you say is OK, Griff.' His eyelids slowly drooped and he lapsed into unconsciousness. The best place for him to be, I figured.

It took me an hour to get him mounted, clear of the town and close by Dutch Hagers' spread. I walked the animals into the front yard and called out his name, but the Dutchman had seen us coming and stepped out on to the narrow stoop, a double-barrelled shotgun in his big hands.

'What you two men want? I got nothing here for you.' He stared up at me, squinting. 'That you, Mr Boone?'

He knew me, I had done him a favour one time in Liberty when he was being rooked out of a cattle deal by some suit from back east. 'I have a wounded man here, Sheriff Winters from Sioux Falls, he has been shot and needs urgent medical attention.'

The big Dutchman propped his gun against the wall

and called for his wife, an equally sizeable woman, and together we lifted the unconscious lawman down from the saddle, into the cabin and on to a cot. I gave them my crude medical kit and the laudanum and asked them to do what they could for him while I rode to Sioux Falls for the doctor, telling them it would probably be early morning before I could get back.

'Don't you worry none, Mr Boone, we will take good care of him.' And I knew that they would.

I rode the mare hard that evening and late into the night, pushing her on across the grassland and taking risks over rocky short cuts I barely remembered but she was game, a sure-footed animal and we arrived sometime after midnight. Sioux Falls was quiet, the oil lamps on Main Street guttering in the gentle evening breeze. I went straight to the sheriff's office and rousted out the night man. An elderly, sleepy-eyed man, a retired deputy I knew as Jed Myers, he staggered from the lock-up area at the back of the stone building where he had been sleeping in an empty cell.

'What the hell you want at this time of night, Boone? Winters is out, he's gone. . . .'

I interrupted him. 'Winters is near dead out at Dutch Hagers' place, he's badly wounded and your two deputies shot to death, I think by the men he went to arrest in Glory. You had best get the doc out there now and then find the livery man, my horse needs attention and I need coffee and some sleep.' The old man stared at me, listening but not hearing. 'Move it, you old bastard, now,' I shouted, my voice raised, angry at his reluctance to move. 'Don't make me tell you again, he's

71

your boss and he needs help like hours ago so move, damn it, move!'

The combination of my voice and the dark look I slapped on him got through to his sleep-filled brain and he dived out of the door while I helped myself to a mug of coffee from the warm pot sitting on top of the small potbellied stove that warmed the office and cells throughout the night. Later, upon reflection, I was saddened by my outburst, the old man was bemused. He was concerned and would suffer greatly later on from the loss of his fellow officers and the possible demise of his boss, but I could not worry about such things in those moments. I needed sleep and found an empty cot in one of the cells – it was still warm, I stripped off my boots and gun belt and, as fatigue overcame me, I sank down on to the cot and was asleep almost as soon as my head hit the black striped tick pillow.

I was up just before sunset, awoken by the old man rattling tin mugs and the smell of freshly-brewed joe. I stamped into my boots and dragged my sore body out into the dim office just as he was turning up the oil lamp. 'Sorry I was so slow to react last night, Griff, I . . .'

'Forget it, Jed, you were half asleep and I was dead beat.'

He looked relieved. 'Doc Watson left about half hour after you got here, him and Gus go way back. Took Deputy Ross and a couple of riders with him and I seen to it your mare was looked after, she looked about as done in as you.'

'Thanks,' I said. 'Good coffee. I have to get back to Liberty, you make sure you wire me as soon as the doc gets back. Will you do that for me?'

'Sure I will. You want some breakfast? I can drum up some bacon and eggs, see you on your way.'

'That would be good, thanks.'

A half hour later I was on my way back across the grassland and heading for Liberty, the morning sun casting a golden bloom across the yellow grass. It was a hard ride on a tired horse but we made it together, that grey mare and me.

It was early evening when we crossed the river and hit the southern boundary of Arrowhead and a starry darkness had engulfed us as we finally reached the crest of the small hill on which I had so often rested when looking down on my property. It was filled with memories, a reassuring view of a good life which had many times been marred with tragedy but never again. It looked promising and that promise I knew was because of the woman, Laura Otis. The mare was lathered and tired. I walked her slowly down and into the yard to be met almost immediately by Henry Mendoza, who took the reins as I leaned forward almost too weary to dismount.

'See to her for me, Henry, the very best – she has carried me around a hundred miles in two days and much of it at speed.' He nodded but did not speak, giving me his strong arm as I stepped down and made my way to the front portico of the house.

Laura suddenly appeared in the doorway, backlit from the lamp inside, then she was running down, off the step and throwing her arms around my neck, burying her face in my shoulder, trembling. 'Where the hell have you been, Griffin Boone? We have been so worried!'

I held her there for a long moment, then gently pushed her away and still holding her, seeing the tears reflected in the lamplight, I held her head in my hands and with my thumbs wiped the tears away. 'Long story, Laura, long story.' And then on an impulse not to be denied, I kissed her moist open mouth, gently but for a long moment. Embarrassed, I stepped back but she pulled my head back down to hers and kissed me again. Then, taking my arm she led me back on to the veranda and into the house, quietly closing the door behind us and turning, kissed me again. She was wearing a light cotton robe patterned with small yellow flowers and it had fallen open to the waist, but she made no effort to cover her breasts and smiled at me. 'It's like kissing a cactus soaked in kerosene, but one more will not hurt me.' And so I kissed her again.

'I will pour you a whiskey, you look like you need one and then I will put some water on to boil, you look and smell like a hobo.'

Laura Otis slept in my arms that night and I in hers. She worked the knots out of my back and massaged the pain from my head, she made me laugh and I made her cry and together we shared a moment that, only a few days before, neither of us had thought we would ever experience again. But there it was, a feeling and a passion shared, driving away the darkness, the loneliness of the past ten years.

The last thing she whispered to me before exhaustion

74

and sleep overcame both of us was, 'Don't you ever ride away from me like that again Griffin Boone, not ever – will you promise me that?'

I made that promise to her, not knowing that within days it would be a promise I would have to break.

CHAPTER SEVEN

THE DARK RIDERS

It was quite a substantial building as line shacks went. Usually they were built for a single line rider and he was expected to maintain it and leave it in good order for the next occupant. A solitary existence mostly, with the cowhand riding the line to see that the cattle he was employed to watch over did not stray from the home range, and to move on any branded strays from neighbouring ranches. The one Ben Logan found had long since been abandoned when the smaller ranches north of Liberty consolidated and it was no longer on any line but part of the history of Will Rider's Rocking Jay, one of the largest ranches in the county. One big, low-ceilinged room with two bunks, a sink, iron hand pump, a rough sawn timber table, chairs, stove and glazed windows. There was a two-holer out the back of the barn and a substantial lean-to built on with a small corral, just large enough for the dozen or so horses it currently held. Bed rolls were spread out in any spare floor space and the place stank of man sweat, lamp oil smoke and saddle leather.

Ben Logan was in a dark mood; he sat on the partially-covered porch with Emilio Vargas watching Smitty rub down his favourite bay horse. Howard Smith was the oldest member of the bunch and had worked with Logan on and off over the years, including the long ride up from New Orleans. He was a good solid man to have in a fight and also, because of his dignified appearance, gentlemanly behaviour and town mode of dress, was an ideal point man to send on any job to observe the layout and ascertain the dangers of any possible venture. You talked to Smitty, you trusted him, respected him and the information he gathered on any reconnoitre always proved invaluable. Flynn though was a different matter altogether.

Ben Logan was accustomed to his orders being obeyed, followed to the letter; Liberty was to be his one big hit before heading back to Louisiana and the tables with Vargas and Smitty, leaving the rest of the gang he had gathered together to do what they did best and live what he suspected would be very short lives without his guidance. Forward thinking and meticulous planning. Now that planning for this last raid was in jeopardy because of one man, the loose cannon that was Huck Flynn.

'You want I should just shoot him?' Vargas asked matter-of-factly, his south-of-the-border soft voice always offering that hint, that strange mixture of humour and deadly intent.

'I would like that, Emilio, I really would like that but maybe I can find another way to rid us of this asshole.' There was a hint of bitterness to the soft Irish burr.

'Why did you send for him? How come you got mixed up with a gringo like that?'

'Long story short?'

'Very short, *amigo*.'

'My first job, a small town of Bright Falls north of Wichita, small town but big, big bank, twice a year, buying and selling time, cattle coming in by the bunch. It was Bat Masterson's idea, he was the Wichita town marshal at the time and he did not welcome the trigger-happy riff raff that came with the cattle in his town. Set up Bright Falls, use it as a turnaround place, a business place, a facility for the cattle buying, the selling and the paying off. Set up a couple of saloons, gaming tables, some whores, you know the kind of things to keep the dusty, dirty, tired and far from home drovers happy for a couple of nights, spend their money and go on home giving Wichita a miss. It was a sound idea, Masterson was no fool. The bank was open from early till late and I decided to hit it in the late evening.'

'So where does Flynn come in?' There was an edge of impatience in the dark man's voice. He sipped his drink, wishing it was tequila, and smoked his last cigarillo.

'There were five of us, five of the Irish brigade.' He chuckled. 'Brigade my eye, a bunch of no-account green outlaws was what we were. Me, Flynn, Pepper Boyd, his brother Jerry and Timothy O'Brian, old Tim – he had a wooden leg, lost the real one in the war – seems about everyone lost a limb in that damned war. Anyways, it was a walk in, walk out job, hit it in the evening, easy, only it wasn't. Masterson was a sharp man, he had the place covered, Bright Falls was an armed camp and ready. Flynn and I went into the bank, the Boyd brothers covered the street and old Tim held the horses on account of his being not very quick on the peg. We got two bags of money but when we came out the shooting started and we were shot to pieces. The Boyd brothers died where they stood, Tim was shot off his horse and his wooden leg stuck in the stirrup, pulling it off, leaving him staggering about in the street, hopping around in that long black coat he wore, a big Colt .45 thumb-buster in each hand, yelling, lost, waving the big pistols until he went down. Seems every gun was turned on him, bits of him flying everywhere. Hell of a sight, like some running jumping scarecrow. In that moment of confusion Flynn grabbed two horses, pulled them to the bank and we lit out. We were both hit but no doubt about it he saved my life that evening.'

'So you owed him, why? You would have done the same for him.'

'Would I? Maybe yes, maybe no.'

'I think so, Logan.'

'We hid out together for a couple of weeks to let our wounds heal then we split up, shared what we had, I headed south to New Orleans and he went to the big city, said Chi would make a change from sagebrush and ticks. I heard he was down on his luck is all.' Logan sat there, his eyes on some past and distant day on a main street in a forgotten town, three dead men and the repeated image of an old one-legged man dancing to the tune of a dozen guns.

Vargas let the moment pass, then got to his feet and went inside. As he passed the thoughtful Logan, his slim fingers touched the man's shoulder and gently squeezed. 'That was a long ago day, Ben, it cannot be changed, compadre, it is what it was and it does no good to dwell on it. I'll get us another sundowner.'

Logan nodded but his thoughts were still out there on the Bright Falls main street and he knew that probably they always would be, one way or another.

Huck Flynn was sipping moonshine from a thick glass jar that had once been filled with peach preserve. He swirled each sip of the fiery drink around his gums before swallowing it noisily. He looked over at the kid, Jimmy Treadwell, whittling away on a piece of dry wood with a horn-handled folding knife, wondering why the boy had felt the urge to shoot the downed and dying deputy. 'Want some, kid? Lightning in a jar, sure hits the spot and keeps the night cold out.'

'No thanks, Huck, I don't have a taste for liquor.'

'You come from one of those temperance families, boy? I heard there are such people.' He chuckled. 'Never knew one yet but they sure enough do march to a band in some towns.'

'No, my daddy was a drinking man, made him do foolish things.'

'Men do foolish things without taking to 'shine or whiskey. Like shooting a dead man for instance, that would be a foolish thing to do, wouldn't you say so, kid?'

'I thought he was moving, could have pulled as he went down.'

'He was dead before he hit the ground, I don't miss.'

'Well maybe. . . .'

'No maybes, kid, you just wanted to know what it was like to shoot a man, to put a round in another man's body, send him to hell and gone. You wanted to get that feeling and you were just a shade too late.'

'Whatever you say, Huck.' The boy stared silently at the ground, moving the wood chips with the toe of his worn-down shoe.

'Don't sulk, boy, I don't like sulking. What's done is done and you will get plenty of chances if you stick with me. I've taken down maybe six men I know of, others maybe in a shootout where you don't know where your round goes or through thick smoke like in the army. Don't worry, you will get your fill of it soon enough.'

'You were in the army?' Treadwell looked across the street to where Logan and the Mexican were sitting and wondered vaguely what the two of them thought of Huck Flynn and him riding in together.

'I served two years before I skedaddled, too much bullshit but I took me down a lot of Johnny Rebs before I left. Half of them didn't have shoes to wear or powder enough left to fight, I could see it was nearly over so I quit and headed west and eventually met up with friend Logan over there, him now cosying up to that damned greaser and shouting at me like I was some kind of border trash.'

'The Mex was pretty damned fast on the pull, fastest I've ever seen.'

81

'You seen a lot of fast guns have you, Jimmy boy?'

'A few, enough to know what is quick and what isn't. Camp fire show-offs mostly although I did see a US marshal named Wes Harper shoot a man down in Billings – he was one of a hell of a fast man on the pull, everyone said, it was something to see.'

'The Shadow Rider, I heard tell of him, killer with a badge is all.'

'I wouldn't know about that but I do know Vargas is quick and we had best steer well clear of him.'

'The hell we will, kid. When this caper is done I intend to settle up with our Mexican friend and remind Ben Logan he would be a dead man were it not for me.'

'How come?'

'Mind your own goddamned business and go over there and bring me another jug.'

Dark, lightning-laced thunder clouds roamed the high peaks beyond Liberty, the deluge they promised swept down over the foothills and soaked the grassland in warm rain. It was hot and uncomfortable in the line shack where several wooden buckets captured water dripping from the leaking ceiling of the old building, the room filled with the seven smoking or playing cards. Logan knew there would be trouble sooner rather than later so he sought to head it off by discussing their venture, the long-planned raid on Liberty's bank. He called the men together around the table and spread out a sheet of paper on the front of which was an old portrait of himself, declaring him to be wanted for robbery and horse theft and offering a $500 reward.

'Terrible likeness there, Ben, you are not that good looking,' Emilio Vargas said. The remark was followed by hoots of laughter; the tension was broken but only temporarily and Logan was aware of that fact.

'The paper on you was so ugly I couldn't bear to bring it, left it on the post office wall to scare the kids,' Logan said, causing more laughter. There was a bond between the two men that the outlaws, with the obvious exception of Huck Flynn, appreciated. 'OK, now settle down.' He turned the paper over revealing a roughly-drawn sketch of Liberty showing the positions of the bank, the sheriff's office, the post and telegraph office, general store, billiard hall, the Black Pony Saloon and the livery stable. 'This is what we have, it's what I remember but in a couple of days we will have a detailed map and your individual roles in the raid. And let me stress,' he fixed Flynn with his cold blue eyes, 'those roles will be followed to the letter. I want you all to think on that and remember. I do not want another Bright Falls on my hands. Are we clear on that?'

There was a murmuring among the group, each fully aware of the dreadful fire brought down on Logan's raiders on that occasion even though it was long before they tied their brands in with his.

'At the end of each month the bank is stuffed with money and even more so this month, not only wages for the local ranches but it is also the last day for the county taxes and that is mostly paid in by cash. You can bet the tight-fisted homesteaders and cattlemen will have left payment until the very last moment. I need to be sure that nothing has changed since I was last through there,

I would hate to hit that bank and only come out with the 500 we are going to pay into it.'

'Our 500?' Harris asked.

'Seed money, Smitty will need it.'

'Why Smitty?' It was Flynn, the man irritable and agitated at being singled out earlier.

'Smitty is presentable, he speaks well, and he is gregarious.'

'Gregarious? What kind of American are we speaking here, boss?' Lomax said.

Logan ignored the question. 'I am sending Mr Smith here into Liberty tomorrow for a couple of days to get the finer details and to ascertain the risks.'

'Ascertain?' Lomax asked.

'Make certain of, find out, learn – hell, Lomax, I'm going to buy you a dictionary out of my cut.' More laughter.

Vargas looked down at the bucket nearest to him, the surface was still; he walked over to the open doorway and looked out. 'It's stopped raining.' he said.

Howard Smith went quietly about his business. A dapper, slim man dressed in a chequered suit, high collared white shirt and his neatly trimmed hair covered by a smart tan derby hat. Over three days he noted the movements of the bank staff and the local law. The former he had met at the bank, introducing himself as Benjamin Smith and depositing $500, the last of the gang's bankroll entrusted to him for that very purpose by Ben Logan. He had several drinks with Seymour Hodge, the bank's head clerk, in Lassiter's Billiard Hall and played a few frames with the rotund little man, who lost every frame but not his propensity to chatter when filled with alcohol.

Smith was relaxed and easy in his way of conversing, a gentleman, knowledgeable and a good listener. He would make a comment, ask a question and just sit back and listen. 'A nice quiet town you have here, Seymour, I cannot stand rowdy places.'

Hodge nodded in agreement, sipping his whiskey and happy to be sitting down and chatting with his new friend – billiards was not his game. 'We have a fine county sheriff, good man, pillar of the community, I doubt he has had to pull his gun in a year or more, wasn't always like that though, Liberty could be rough.'

'I have not seen him around,' Smith said.

'Down with the fever,' Hodge said.

'Nothing serious I hope?'

'No, his old lady fusses too much.'

'He has a good deputy then I guess.'

'Two of them, one permanent and one part-time.'

'Not met them either.'

'Joe Ross, the permanent man, is not a mixer, he mostly leaves it to the part-timer Griffin Boone and Griff seems more interested in what is going down over in Sioux Falls.'

'Oh?'

'Sioux Falls, the Sioux County seat about forty miles or so south east of here.'

'What's the interest over there?' Smith waved at the barman who nodded and sent over two more drinks.

'Mighty nice of you, Mr Smith.'

'Benjamin, please.'

'Benjamin it is then . . . well, it seems the sheriff over there got himself all shot up a few days back, real bad trouble.'

'That trouble is not heading this way, I hope.'

'No, sir, you can rest assured on that score. Seems he got himself and a couple of deputies shot up real bad when they got themselves bushwhacked by a gang of gunsels from the east. Passing through most likely and long gone by now. Two peace officers killed and the sheriff badly wounded, nasty business all around.'

'Why is your man so interested?'

'He set the Sioux Falls people on the alert, feels it was his fault. It wasn't of course but he is that kind of a man.'

'I would like to meet him.'

'You will if you are here long enough and especially if you decide to set up a business in Liberty.'

'I like it already, Seymour, I think it quite likely I will be visiting your bank again shortly for a withdrawal and maybe even a loan.'

CHAPTER EIGHT

NASHVILLE

Laura Otis and Chuck were in town, driven there in the buggy by Henry Mendoza, she to shop for I know not what and Chuck in the hope that Henry would show him more of the sights and maybe buy him some candy. Bill Ross was happy to cover the morning shift and I promised to be in town by lunchtime so that we could all have a meal together at the Chinaman's. That left me with the morning to sort out my county tax bill and do some other paper chores, jobs I hated but were very necessary when running a moderately-sized cattle ranch. Will Rider, my neighbour over at the much larger Rocking Jay, employed a lady bookkeeper, a handsome woman named Elsa Reese who it was said spent one heck of a lot of her time bookkeeping at the Rocking Jay – small town chit-chat. She had offered me her services but I had declined and, sometimes like now, looking at a heap of papers, I wished that maybe I should have accepted her help. Some of my stock books were still kept in the bedroom I had allocated to Laura and I needed them. She had rarely used the room since the night of my return from Sioux Falls but it was still, in every sense of the word, her room, her private space and I excused myself in that it was a very necessary intrusion for which I would later apologize. The room was neat and tidy, it smelled of perfume and fresh linen, Laura's smell. I opened the pine chest by the window, took out the books I needed and left; as I passed her dressing table I could not help but notice the silver-framed picture standing beside her perfume spray, hairbrush and comb. Two people in much the same pose as the one of Martha and I, a stiff-backed young man in the butternut grey of the Army of Northern Virginia and a young and quite lovely Laura Otis. There was something oddly familiar about the handsome young man and it puzzled me greatly. I stared at it for a long time, studied upon it, desperately reaching back and quite suddenly a great coldness rippled along my spine. I shivered, my neck hairs spiked, my leg began to throb and I quit the room.

General John Bell Hood of the Texas Brigade and the Army of Tennessee was a man of many parts and also a man who had shed a lot of his own blood during the five years he served Robert E. Lee in the Civil War. Wounded, he lost the use of an arm at Gettysburg, a leg at Chickamauga and his sense of humour somewhere between the two. I served with him from brigade commander to general without a scratch until the Christmas

Eve of 1865, a few days after the last big fight on the Western Theatre, the Battle of Nashville. I was part of the rear-guard covering our route and retreat along the Granny White Pike where we destroyed the Duck River Crossing and slowed down the Federal pursuit, allowing the remnants of the Army Of Northern Virginia to escape across the Tennessee River. But even then it really was just about all over and shortly thereafter General Lee surrendered at Appomattox Court House. But it wasn't the end for me, at least not the one I had envisaged.

'Come on, boys,' I yelled waving my sabre, my empty pistol holstered for lack of powder and shot, riding back and forth among the soldiers as we crossed the Duck River. 'Blow her high and wide, lads.'

Those of us who were the last to make it across counted ourselves lucky and me most of all. I had thought for a while there at that very moment I might make it through the war after all, but a couple of Federal sharpshooters on the far bank put an end to that fantasy and peppered me with Minie balls. Three rounds hit my right leg, two of which went clean through, killing the horse under me. My boys (and like me in many ways, they were boys) got me to a field hospital and I lay there on a blood-wet stretcher for nigh on two hours before a surgeon reached me. He was a youngster wearing a blood encrusted apron, he was blue of eye and steady of hand. He cut my pants away and examined the wounds, he looked at me and then off at the pile of arms and legs protruding from beneath a grey tarpaulin, studying them for a long moment before turning back to me and asking, 'What is your name, soldier?'

'Griffin Boone, captain under the command of John Bell Hood, and it does not hurt so badly now, it has gone kind of numb.'

'It's a bad one, Captain, ragged and the bone is shot to hell and gone.' Again he looked over to the ghastly fly-blown heap of arms and legs and then back at me. 'But I will be damned if I will cut off another limb this day.' He signalled to a nearby stretcher bearer. 'Get some help and get this man on to my table now.' He winked at me and walked back into the blood-stinking field station.

I remembered clearly to this very day listening to his softly spoken reassuring words, saying thank you before fainting away from the pain I had so determinedly thought to deny.

I never saw him again, that young surgeon; I was told when the laudanum-induced delirium had passed, that he had patched me up and taken care of me for three days and nights before being transferred with his unit to Richmond. Not seen him, that is, until I had stumbled upon the photograph of him that morning on the dressing table of Laura Otis.

The cottonwood grove was as peaceful as ever, a gentle breeze moving the long grass that surrounded it, disturbing the bees that gathered upon the masses of waving, bright red Indian paintbrush. I removed the wilting flowers of the previous day placed there by Maria and replaced them with those I had gathered from the small garden out back of the house that Martha had so lovingly cared for. It was and always would be a heavy-eyed moment for me. Should we have remained in Texas? Would she have caught the fever had we stayed? Imponderables, unanswerable questions, fleeting moments of misery and uncertainty. Would she approve of my growing fondness for Laura Otis? I believed that she would.

I did not hurry my ride into Liberty; in the first place I was riding an unfamiliar horse, a feisty chestnut, having been persuaded by Mendoza to give the mare a rest and secondly I felt it right to give Laura freedom to negotiate the varied and many nuances of the town without my standing behind her. I paused once for twenty minutes or so by the cold chattering water of Liberty Creek giving me just enough time to haul four good-sized crappies from the clear water, fish I thought I would persuade the Chinaman to cook for our supper before we headed back to Arrowhead in the evening. He had the art and skill of turning an ordinary fish supper into something oriental and delicate without losing the real freshwater flavour of the wild fish.

The livery stable was cool and I asked the duty man to feed the chestnut and check out his front left hoof which, from the awkwardness of the animal's gait, was carrying a loose shoe. From there I made several calls, dropped the fish off at the Dead Duck Café, touched the brim of my hat to the ladies, picked up mail from the post office and several wires from the telegraph station before sitting down behind my desk and, after hearing his report that all was well, sending Bill Ross

91

home for the day.

Seymour Hodge the bank manager dropped by and introduced me to his new friend Benjamin Smith, an investor from the east wanting to open a business in Liberty.

'Good to meet you, sir,' I said, remembering that Sawyer had told me it was my civic duty to the town to welcome any newcomers with money to spend. Smith looked the part in his brown chequered suit and derby hat. 'What made you choose Liberty?'

'I heard it was a nice quiet town, Sheriff,' Smith said.

'It is,' I said.

'I like quiet towns,' Smith said.

'Then you came to the right place. What business are you in?'

'I'm a barber.'

'We already have a barber.'

'I know, Jake Williams, an old man, he wants to move on, sell out but I need to check the area out first.'

'Jake never mentioned that to me,' Hodge said.

'Why should he? I asked him to keep it on the quiet until I made up my mind.'

'And have you?' Hodge said. 'Made up your mind?'

'Nearly, this territory becomes a state as they say it will then Liberty will be a growing town being right slap bang in the middle and all.'

'Well, good luck with that, Mr Smith, I will not breathe a word of it.'

'Thank you, sheriff, I will be seeing you around no doubt. I could trim that moustache up for you a little and maybe take some of the grey out of the temples – I specialize in such matters, not just a regular haircutter is all.'

We shook hands again and he left, I watched them cross the street to the Black Pony, got out from behind the desk and studied my reflection in the small chipped mirror that hung on the wall. Damn it, there was grey at the temples and my moustache could stand a trim. I wondered had Laura noticed that and guessed that she had.

The mail on my desk was of little interest, a few fliers of wanted men we were unlikely to see and a reminder that county taxes were due at the end of the month. I thought of Heck Thomas and my promise to call on him, making a mental note that I would try to fit it in as soon as possible and then wondering if he had settled his tax bill and doubting he had. One of the wires was interesting and it was the one I had hoped to see. It was from Doc Watson in Sioux Falls: Gus Winters still critical but out of danger, very poorly, you saved his life for sure and we all thank you for that. I rocked back in my chair thinking my impulsive ride to Glory had been an instinctive and correct call. But that did not alter the fact that the killers were still on the loose and I wondered where they were at that moment. Clear of Wyoming? Running down to Colorado or, my best guess if they were smart, way to the north, Montana and over the border and into Canada?

I was still thinking on that when Laura and Chuck darkened my doorway and breezed into the office. 'Busy, deputy?' she said, smiling that smile, a broad smile I was used to, not the coy hint of a smile she wore in the photograph on the bedroom dressing table. 'If not will you do me a favour?'

'Sure, what can I do for you, ma'am? I am here to serve and protect.'

'I like that, you should make that the slogan of your office.'

'You think?' I said.

'Yes, I think,' she said.

'So what is the favour?'

'Take care of Charlie for an hour or so, he's at a loose end, Henry had some business in the saloon and I need to see about becoming a schoolteacher – girl talk.' She rolled her eyes.

'Sure,' I said, 'be happy to.'

She blew me a kiss, flattened the boy's blond hair and left. The boy looked at me, ruffled his hair again and rolled his eyes. Like mother like son, I thought.

Charlie Otis was a bright kid, he asked a lot of kid questions and listened to the adult answers, making I guess his own judgement as to the reliability of those answers based on his knowledge of the adult giving them. I liked having him around and hoped my answers were adjudged to be reliable. He spent quite a lot of time in either mine or Henry Mendoza's company, something Laura had asked for, feeling he had spent too much of his young life around women who wanted to ruffle his hair and that he needed to be more in the company of grown men. Both Henry and I were flattered that she believed we fitted that role.

'What's new, Chuck?' I asked, pushing the papers on my desk to one side and giving him my full attention.

He stared back at me, thoughtful, a little apprehensive. 'There is a Red Indian down by the post office, sir, sitting on the porch, he told me he is a friend of yours and to go away. He is very old I think, maybe a Sioux, I do not see that he is carrying a tomahawk.'

I got to my feet and walked to the door, looked across at the post office to where an old Indian in worn buckskins, his silver hair braided with a coloured band, was sitting on a wooden tilted chair, resting on the back two legs. I went back and sat on the front edge of the desk. 'He wouldn't be carrying a weapon except maybe a knife or a hunting rifle. His name is Walking Horse and he is a Crow Indian, used to be an army scout up north but he retired and moved down south to here. He does some tracking for the county sometimes, say maybe a big cat moves down from the high country and worries the cattle, well then we call on Walking Horse and he takes care of it for us.'

'He have a first name, Mr Boone?'

I shook my head. 'Indians do not usually have first names in the way we do so we call him Billy, and he doesn't mind that.'

'Why did he move south?'

'Tell you what, Chuck, why don't we walk on over there and ask him just that, I always wondered myself why he did that.'

'You sure he is a friend of yours? He was not too friendly toward me, said I woke him up but his eyes were not closed so I thought he was awake.'

'He was probably just thinking and meant you disturbed him. I'll wear my gun so he can see we mean business.' I smiled inwardly; Billy Walking Horse was just about the most peaceable man I had ever come across. 'Come on, let's go meet him.'

We clunked our way along the dried hard wood of the sidewalk to where Billy Walking Horse was seated, his chair still rocked back, his eyes closed. The boy stood tight against my right leg and moved a little closer when Billy opened one eye and looked hard at him.

'That nosy kid a friend of yours, Boone?' His voice was husky and deep.

'He is,' I said.

'He thinks I am an Apache,' he said.

'No, he thinks you are a Sioux,' I said.

'You tell him I don't like the Sioux, that's why I moved south.'

'No. You tell him, he also wanted to know why you moved south.'

'Like I said, a nosy kid.' He closed his eyes again but I could see the trace of a smile on his grizzled weather-beaten face.

'He also wonders why you don't carry a tomahawk.'

'Anything else he wonders about? Has he lost his tongue?'

'No he is just a bit nervous of you, he is from the east.'

'Oh, that explains that then.'

'I am going to leave him here with you while I do a couple of chores, you can tell him all about yourself and how you counted coup on the yellow-haired general one time.'

'I said I did that?'

'You did.'

'I might of made that up.' He set the chair down on all four legs and opened his eyes, looked directly at Chuck. 'You want to hear some stories, kid?'

'Yes, sir,' Chuck said, moving away from my leg and sitting down on the step-up to the sidewalk. 'I would like that.'

'See you both in a little while then.' I flattened his hair as his mother had done and left the two of them sizing each other up.

That evening before setting out for Arrowhead we had supper at the Dead Duck Café, where Kang had prepared the bass in some sort of light batter with a strong, sweet seasoning which was pleasant on the palate, but left me wondering if spit roasted crappies over an open camp fire would not have tasted just that thin edge better. I mentioned this to Laura and she scolded me a little, saying it was good to try new things. Henry Mendoza had taken the chestnut back to the ranch, leaving me to drive the buggy and I was happy that it worked out that way. It was a star-filled sky of a Wyoming night and even the constant breeze had dropped away to almost nothing. Chuck, wrapped in a blanket, was fast asleep between us, probably dreaming, his head filled with the wonderful lies of Billy Walking Horse. Laura sang a song about wild mountain thyme, a Scottish ballad with which I was not familiar but immediately loved. She had a deep contralto voice so sweet and true that any musical accompaniment would have been an intrusion. I took that ride home to be one of the most joyous and peaceful rides I had ever taken. Once the memory of the photograph crossed my mind and I supressed the urge to mention it, feeling it not to be the right moment for either of us but especially not for me.

The next few days were peaceful and the three of us shared the afternoons together, riding, walking and fishing. Laura was a mean angler and quick to gut the fish and prepare them on a campfire put together by the boy while I supervised from beneath the shade of a cottonwood. Joe Sawyer was back part-time and worked the morning shift, mostly with either Ross or I taking over mid-afternoon. A further wire from Sioux Falls reassured us that Gus Winters was well on the road to recovery and I would be welcome for a visit, time permitting. One brief but lovely afternoon I showed them to a small, secluded valley on the north of my property and as we mounted a low hill and looked down upon the long grass, I enjoyed the gasp of surprise from both Laura and Chuck as they watched a small herd of buffalo grazing the valley bottom, the great shaggy beasts seemingly unaware of our presence.

'Survivors,' I said, 'the last of the few.'

'They are beautiful,' Laura said, taking my hand and sharing the moment.

'Billy told me there were millions of them one time and that now they have all gone,' Chuck said. 'I guess he does not know of these?'

'He knows,' I said. 'It was he who found them.'

'Can I tell him I have seen them?' Chuck said.

'Yes, but no one else, is that a deal?'

'Yes, sir, a deal.' He spat on his hand and offered it to me. I spat on mine and took it, much to Laura's eye-

98

rolling amusement.

And those precious moments were the end of the good times for what seemed a long while.

The next day, Friday, I was working at my desk reading the local paper, Laura was shopping with Maria and Chuck was outside on the boardwalk practising mumbley-peg with a clasp knife I had bought him, a generous act I thought, not reckoning on the scolding Laura had given me for buying him a knife without asking her first – after all, she insisted, he was only ten years old. I held back from telling her that my daddy had given me a Bowie knife when I was only nine. I was halfway through the editorial when I heard the terrified scream from Chuck followed by gunshots. I grabbed my gun from the holster hanging on the back of my chair and made the doorway in two quick strides. Chuck was on his knees, looking up at me wild-eyed and terrified. I reached for him as I turned my attention to Main Street, the bank and a vaguely familiar figure with a revolver in his hand. I tried to throw the boy behind me but before I could reach him I was smacked in the head by a giant fist, I staggered and was hit again. I reached out for a porch upright as the world around me turned upside down and a great darkness overcame me, pitching me down into an even darker world filled with a young boy screaming, hoof beats and ragged gunshots, all fading to a distant murmur.

CHAPTER NINE

THE RAIDERS

Ben Logan was never the same after the massacre at Bright Falls, it had been his fault and he accepted that responsibility. Dead men in the street: his doing not by his gun but because he had not planned well enough ahead, had not foreseen the possibilities, he had badly underestimated Bat Masterson – it would never happen again. After splitting trails with Huck Flynn a weary Logan had ridden south, hard and long to New Orleans as far away from Kansas as he could. Still aching from his wounds and nearly broke he spent what little money he had left on a second-hand suit of clothes, a derby hat and town shoes. Suitably attired, he asked for and was given a dealer's job on the Silver Queen, a middle-range river boat catering for low stakes gamblers. He dealt faro and blackjack mostly, he played a fair game and was popular amongst the ladies who also plied their trade on the Queen as well as the rubes who flashed their money away on impossible hands. Management were also keen to have him on duty as he had a gentle way with handling troublemakers and bad losers, of which there were many.

Ben Logan learned one hell of a lot on the Silver Queen but most of all he learned something about himself. He was a born gambler. When not working the cards on the Queen, he was winning or losing earnings in one gambling joint or another in the city itself. On either side of the green baize he needed the feel of the Bicycle cards in his slim-fingered hands. It did not seem to matter whether or not the money was the Queen's or his own, the beast had to be fed.

Broke and sitting in his quarters, supper finished, sipping bourbon courtesy of management and awaiting another payday, Logan convinced himself that the problem was he never had quite enough money for the big stake. He knew himself to be an excellent poker player but how many times, he asked himself, had he had to quit, fold a winning hand because his poke was empty? The solution was obvious; if he wanted to satisfy the burning hunger for a royal flush he needed that one big stake, that one big hand then, the inevitable gambler's promise to himself, he could quit once and for all. Work would not get him that stake and neither would playing five-card stud for nickels and dimes in a downtown New Orleans gambling hall.

It came to him slowly as good ideas often do. Bright Falls was a catastrophe but it need not have been; careful planning was the key, that and, just as it had been in the war, intelligence gathering. An observant man over a period of days would have spotted the opposition, the dangers so inherent in such a venture. That was the key, that was the first step on the short road back to one Bright Falls or another.

A good poker player, a winning gambler, is a shrewd judge of men – he has to be, the backs of a deck of Bicycle playing cards tell him nothing but watch the man who is holding them, fingering them. Watch the man's eyes, his lips, the odd tic, the movement of his fingers, his shoulders, the way he holds his glass, his voice, the way he lights a stogie.

A regular at Logan's table on the Queen was a tall, handsome man of mixed blood. Mexican for sure but with a large touch of the Irish about him. His name was Emelio Vargas although he sometimes introduced himself as Milo O'Brian, usually then with a bright white-toothed smile. Logan was drawn to him right away. The sense of humour, the grace with which he lost, a frequent occurrence. The way he folded and left the table knowing he probably had the better hand but, like Logan, not the money to back the play. The precise way he spoke.

'How much did you drop tonight, Emilio?' Logan asked, joining the Irish Mexican at the long bar. The tables were shut down, the green baize covered, crew members, mostly black men, sweeping the decking and emptying the over-laden ash trays. The passengers and gamblers retired to their rooms and, as the boat rocked to a slight swell as she headed back for New Orleans, the rhythm of the big stern wheel sending them to sleep, a quiet time for the weary dealers and a few of the ladies gathered at the bar.

'You were not card counting tonight, my friend? You are always counting.' He laughed.

'I am,' Logan said.

'How long have you been on the river?'

'Six months.'

'A long time and you are still not a winner?'

'Excuse me?' Logan said.

'I often see you playing the cards ashore, you play right but you are not a big winner yet.'

'I mostly do OK.'

'I do not believe so but I am sorry, it is none of my business.'

'It's a game, just a game is all it is.'

'They pay you well to run a table on the riverboat?'

'Not too well but it is free accommodation, the food is better than good and the players chip in generously if they win and the ladies are friendly.'

'Very friendly if you have the money . . . but are there not other ways for a man of your talents to win at cards?'

'I play a straight game, Emilio, you know that, here on board or in town, it makes no difference. There is no satisfaction in winning if you are playing in a crooked game,' Logan said.

'No offence meant, señor, it was just a thought is all.'

'And a thought I do have from time to time,' Logan said, laughing and touching glasses with Vargas. 'There are many other ways to win though, without a deck of cards.'

'Tell me about those many other ways.'

And that is how it began for Ben Logan, the road

back to a Bright Falls in any other name.

Two weeks later Ben Logan and his new companion Emilio Vargas crossed the Louisiana line and rode into the East Texas border country. Logan was still wearing his derby hat. Turning north before reaching San Antonio they hit a bank in Harpersville and another in the small township of Valence, raising what Logan referred to as 'seed money'. Along the way they had also picked up a fellow traveller and old friend of Logan's, Howard J. Smith, a tall dapper man who could not have looked less like a bank robber but who in fact was good at his chosen task of point man, checking ahead to see that there was likely to be only a minimum of interference from the law and not too much chance of a hot pursuit.

In the small town of Brooks Wells, a yellow-haired young man with a tied down Colt Frontier took exception to the dark-skinned Vargas drinking at what he claimed to be a white man's bar and told him that people of colour were not welcome. When Vargas laughed at him, he pulled but Vargas shot him in the shoulder before the weapon cleared the holster causing the youngster to cap the round and shoot himself in the foot. The boy would walk with a limp for the rest of his life but at least he was alive and several witnesses gave testimony to the fact that it was a sure case of self-defence. It seemed to Logan that the kid was not the most popular inhabitant of Brooks Wells. Nevertheless, the town marshal suggested it best the trio moved on and that they did. Still heading north toward the Panhandle they picked up a fourth man, Tom Harris, a good man with horses, mostly other people's stock. He was also handy with a gun and happy to use one. The four of them hit a post office in Silverton before crossing into Colorado at the northern Sherman County line.

Harris took care of the twelve-horse remuda they had gathered along the way, seeing to the needs of the animals and tying them off to a night line.

Five nights later, the four men clasping hot coffee mugs huddled around a sparking campfire, the Texas nights without warning having turned bitterly cold.

'You are some fast gun, Emilio.' It was the first time the shooting had been mentioned and Logan had kept his own counsel on the matter, but now felt it needed airing.

'No, he was just very slow,' Vargas said.

'Did you mean to wound him or to kill him?'

'Either way was all right I guess.'

'I don't hold with killing,' Logan said. 'I never have.'

'What difference would it have made to anything if I had killed him?'

'It would have made a difference to me, Emilio, we rob banks, we are looking for a stake is all, we will be forgotten, small fry, but you kill a man and people remember. They get excited, post rewards and suddenly we are running faster than we intended with nowhere to rest. So far, other than a warning shot or two, we have not capped a round in anger and I want it to stay that way.'

'Do not worry, my friend, I will not jeopardize our mission, a bank clerk or a lawman, no, but a kid with a gun is of no consequence to me. If it makes you happy though, I shot to wound him, he gave me enough time for that. Had he been faster, well then I do not know.'

Logan burst out laughing, coughing on his stogie. 'Damn young fool shot himself in the foot, did you see his face? Damnedest thing I ever saw!'

Then all four of them were laughing.

After a brief stopover in Green River where Logan bought three more horses and wired Huck Flynn, he took on a new man, a no-account gunfighter known mostly as Chad Lomax although several wanted posters throughout Colorado featuring his likeness gave him a different name. He was an associate of Tom Harris. With the two new gang members in tow they skirted Denver and crossed from Colorado into Wyoming, riding hard across Arrowhead land and headed for the ghost town of Glory.

The big sky was a clear blue, no hint of rain or storm clear to the mountains beyond. The men were gathered around as before with Logan at the table and a new map to show. 'This is with the compliments of Mr Smith who gathered this intelligence and also confirms the safe should be full on Friday and there will only be a part-time deputy on hand. No bank guards and no militia standing by. The part-time bank guard is usually gone before it closes, leaving only a cashier and the chief clerk who is usually in the Black Pony until lockdown time. There has never been an attempt on the bank and they are confident that it will remain that way. After all, it isn't their money so why should they worry? I want you to study this map carefully, it outlines your positions and the town itself to a much greater degree of accuracy than the previous map. Take a look and ask questions if you have any.' He stood away from the table and gave them space and time.

Flynn was the first to speak. 'Why am I holding the horses?'

'Because it's what you do best, Huck,' Logan said.

'I would prefer to go in the bank with you and the Mex,' Flynn said.

'No, you hold the horses in the alleyway next to the sheriff's office as planned. Smitty, you keep watch on the street from the saloon, any sign of trouble you signal me and we call the whole thing off there and then.'

'Are we just backup?' asked Lomax.

'Yes, Chad, anything goes wrong you and Tom step in, covering fire if needed but no killing, is that clearly understood?' He let the question hang there for a moment then turned toward Flynn. 'That clear, Huck, we do not want to leave any bodies on the street, theirs or ours.'

'What about the kid, what's his job?'

'He's with you, I don't know anything about him so that makes him your responsibility.'

'I'll be OK, Mr Logan, you can count on that.'

'Good, then are we all clear?'

There was a muttering of agreement.

'We ride at six tomorrow, that means we should be in Liberty just before eight when the bank is due to close. Smitty will ride in first and take up his station opposite the bank, double-checking for any additional security.

Smitty is known to the chief cashier. Vargas and I will follow close behind and go into the bank alone – it should be empty at that time. We should be in the safe before lockdown and then get out fast. We mount up and ride back to where Tom has built a brush corral which will hold our remounts. We change horses and he leads the tired string north to the higher rocky ground and hopefully takes the posse with him.'

'Then where?' Flynn again.

'We also take the high ground but we go east, where the trail will be hard if not impossible to follow, then we swing south to the line shack, rest up for the night and in the morning head back for Glory – that's the last place they will expect to find us. My guess is they will think we are long gone from Wyoming Territory. We lay up there for a couple of days then split the money and ride our separate ways. Is there anything else?' Logan fixed his attention on Flynn but the big man ignored him and followed by the kid, he quit the room.

It was going to be a fine evening and the men rode six abreast across the grassland to the north of Liberty. They paused for smokes and a drink by the brush corral hidden in a cottonwood stand, while Harris checked on the remuda there and watched as Howard Smith rode on ahead.

Smith checked his horse in at the livery as had been his habit over the past week, unsaddled the animal, and then neatly folding his duster and tying it behind his saddle he made his way across to the Black Pony and a drink with Seymour Hodge. The banker greeted him enthusiastically. They chatted about cattle prices and the possibility of Wyoming becoming a state, with Smith keeping a sharp eye on the large wooden-framed clock above the bar. At five to eight he excused himself saying he needed a breath of fresh air. Hodge followed him outside telling him he had to relieve the duty cashier and shut down the bank for the night. Smith nodded and lit a cheroot, leaned against an upright and studied Main Street. Nothing unusual, no activity that drew his sharp attention. He watched Hodge cross the street and enter the bank and noted that Lomax and Harris were both in position opposite the bank, seated on chairs in front of the closed general store. The street was pretty much deserted, save for a kid playing mumbley-peg on the sidewalk outside of the darkened sheriff's office. He blew a smoke ring into the still evening air and touched his hat.

Logan examined the street from the alleyway before handing the reins of his horse over to the kid. He winked at him, the boy smiled. Flynn was surly as he took Vargas' horse.

'Easy now, boys, remember this is the big one,' Logan said.

The two men followed Hodge into the bank, pulling their bandannas over their faces as they did so. Hodge turned, startled by their sudden appearance. Behind the grill the duty cashier immediately raised his hands above his head, showing them to be empty and clear of the counter.

'Easy, fella' Logan said, 'all we want is the money, no trouble, give it over easy and we will be gone. Not your money and not worth either of you dying for.' His voice was soft, the Irish brogue persuasive, calming.

'Yes, sir, yes, sir.' Hodge's voice was little above a whisper.

'The safe, get the money, in bags, nothing loose,' Logan said.

'Yes, sir.' Hodge did not move and Vargas stepped forward and prodded him with his gun. The man trembled and moved quickly to the big safe, reached in and withdrew two large leather bags and a smaller canvas one, handing them to Logan, his hands shaking.

'Down on the floor, both of you,' Vargas said, as they backed toward the door.

'The hell with this,' Flynn said. Irritated at being left in the alley with the horses, he gave the reins to Treadwell and stepped around the corner of the bank and came face to face with Charlie Otis. The boy looked up and screamed in fear, recognizing his mother's tormenter from their first day in the valley.

So easy, thought Logan, then hearing the strangled scream from out on the street and Flynn shouting, swearing, his voice raised and angry followed by two quick pistol rounds.

Hearing the child's scream, the deputy leapt from the doorway of the jail and Flynn shot him twice in the head. The badge tried to regain his feet but before Flynn could fire again, Vargas was shoving him to one side as he ran to the alleyway and the horses with Logan still in the bank and several yards behind him.

Then Hodge was diving for cover, pushing the old cashier out of the way and coming up with the sawn-off shotgun the bank guard stored under the counter when he was not on duty, cocking the piece and firing in the direction of the startled outlaws, the buck shot going high and wide blasting a hole in the ceiling, covering the room in dust and rubble. Vargas was already clear and out of the door, followed by Logan, the man half blinded by the nearness of the shotgun's muzzle flash, dropping two of the bags as he stumbled out on to the street.

Lomax and Harris fired warning shots as men poured from the Black Pony Saloon, sending them back inside, falling over one another in a tangled heap.

Flynn grabbed the kid and holding him to his chest used his slight frame for cover, dragged him back to the restless horses, grabbed a set of reins from Treadwell's shaking hands and still clasping the boy, swung aboard the nearest horse. Logan and Vargas were already mounted and Lomax and Harris ran across the street to join them. Within seconds all six men were heading out of town at a gallop; even as they passed him Logan saw the bloody, half blinded deputy still trying to regain his feet before falling away, rolling off the sidewalk and face down into the dust.

Howard Smith joined the men piling back into the Black Pony, diving under the nearest table with his hands over his ears. Something had gone terribly wrong and he had no wish to be part of the melee in the street or victim of the anger that would surely follow.

CHAPTER TEN

THE PURSUIT

There is a very dark place in the universe, far out of reach and beyond the comprehension of man and somehow I had found it. An unconscious man one minute and awake the next is not how it works and I have no idea how long that darkened gap lasted or when I regained any understanding of real time or what was going on around me. I was down so deep it must have taken me hours to surface. I know this because of later events but at the time, that moment of struggling out of the seeming reality of one darkness to another darkness, a realization of my being Griffin Boone was sudden but in fact had taken hours. My first recollection was of the scent of Laura and the muted sound of her voice; my second the voice of Doc Philburgh as he tried to reassure me that the headache would dissipate and the laudanum would not be needed for the rest of my life and my protestation at its removal was an unnecessary outburst. My head felt like there was thunder

112

rolling around inside my skull and the lightning flashed every time I opened my eyes. My vision was hazy, the swirling room appeared to be filled with smoke that drifted in patches. Clouds in a room? Then slowly, very slowly, I became aware of my state of being, the man beyond the pain, the desire to move, to know my legs still worked. My need to know that I could see beyond the smoke and hear above the roaring in my ears.

'Stay still, Griff, I have to get these stitches in your noggin, I have stopped the bleeding but the wounds need sewing up or it will start all over again.'

'Wounds?' I said.

'Two deep creases over your ear, inch apart, you look a mess, it's going to be hell wearing a hat for a while.'

'The boy,' I said. 'Where is Chuck?'

The scent of her much closer then. 'He took him, the man out by the wagon, Flynn, he took him.'

'I have to go,' I said.

'You cannot go anywhere for a day or so, you would fall out of the saddle within a hundred yards, I guarantee it. The posse are out after them, Joe Sawyer is leading it, you couldn't do anything he can't do,' Philburgh said, pushing me back down on to the cot.

'They need me,' I said.

'They will do fine without you this morning.'

'Morning?'

'You have been out of it for a while, Griff,' Laura said, taking my hand and holding it to her cheek. I could feel her face was swollen and as she leaned over me, I tasted the salt of her tears. I struggled to sit up but she pushed me down. Henry Mendoza took her place and held me

113

while the doc finished the stitching and as the laudanum took effect, I floated away again and thought I could hear her singing the Scottish ballad she had sung that star-filled night only a few days – or was it a lifetime? – ago.

It was late afternoon when I finally awoke to the smell of fresh coffee, my thoughts tangled as I lay there contemplating the events of earlier, trying to get them in line, in some sort of order. My head hurt with the discomfort of Philburgh's stitches tugging at the edges of the wounds but the pain was bearable. I reached up to feel the swollen temple but my hand was pushed away by the doctor. 'Keep your dirty fingers away from there, you want to see it I'll get you a mirror.'

'I have one,' Laura said, sitting beside the cot in what I recognized to be Philburgh's small back room. Her voice was hoarse, throaty I guessed from crying.

She held a mirror close to my head, I adjusted it slightly. The wounds were ragged and flecked with dried blood but neatly stitched and closed. The temple was heavily bruised, dark and ugly.

'Can I sit up?' I said.

'If you are able,' Philburgh said. 'Gently and slowly though.'

I pushed myself to my elbows and then supported by Laura's strong arms, I sat up and swung my legs over the cot's side and settled my feet squarely on to the carpeted floor. 'I seem to have lost my boots,' I said.

'Hang on, I'll get them for you but do not bend down.'

'Why not?'

114

'OK, please yourself, bend down.' He tossed the boots to my distant feet, I leaned forward, felt the floor rushing up to me and hard contact was stopped only by the quick actions of Laura and the doctor grabbing me and pushing me back on to the cot. 'See what I mean?'

'Why are doctors always so damned smart?' I said, fixing my eyes on the oil lamp and regaining my equilibrium.

'I don't know, Griff, we just are, must be all of those years of practice at being so smart.'

'Here, have some coffee. Careful though, it's very hot.' Laura took her arm from around my shoulders and handed me a mug of sweet, steaming joe.

We sat like that, the three of us in the quiet of the little room, the pair of them I guess waiting for me to speak – but I had nothing to say, just questions that I was too afraid to ask.

'You were damned lucky, Griff, either of those shots could have taken your head off were they an inch to the right,' Philburgh said, breaking the silence. 'You rest up for a while, I am not going to even attempt to tell you for how long, that is up to you. Slow and easy is my advice though.'

'Thanks, Doc,' I said. 'Tell me what happened and what is happening now.'

Doc Philburgh was not a great talker and filled me in without embellishments. Six men were involved in the fracas, they tried to rob the bank. Three had been identified for certain from current fliers as Chad Lomax, a gun for hire; Tom Harris, a horse thief and a Mexican named Emilio Vargas wanted in connection with several shootings south of the Picketwire. Another was possibly Huck Flynn, wanted in connection with killing two deputies in Glory. No one was hurt but Seymour Hodge took a chunk out of the bank's ceiling with a scattergun, the thieves dropped most of the money and only got away with around $500 in bills and a kidnapped boy. It was thought that was where it all went south, when Charlie recognized one of the gunmen and alerted me. The man who grabbed the boy for cover was the man who shot me.

'Laura tells us his name is Flynn, Huck Flynn, you had a run-in with him one time and he is likely the man who gunned down Gus Winters in Glory and like as not killed his two deputies.'

'The other men?'

'No idea.'

'And now?'

'The posse got back an hour or so ago, they were dead beat – they found where the gang changed horses but that's about all. They will go out again first light,' he said, looking at me, expecting me, I supposed, to leap to my feet, buckle on my Colt and stagger out to find a horse but I knew that was not the way to go. I doubt that I would have made it to the door.

'Did Billy Walking Horse go with them?'

'No, no one is sure where Billy is,' he said.

'Send a rider out to the Half Moon, Heck Thomas' place, Billy goes there when he needs some 'shine. Tell him what happened, tell him that I need him here pronto, send Henry Mendoza if he's still in town – he can find his way there in the dark.' I turned to Laura.

'What horse did I ride in? I can't seem to remember.'

'The big sorrel,' she said.

'Then ask him to bring me my mare after he has found Billy.'

'You are going after them?' she said.

'You're damned right I am,' I said.

'You need rest first.'

'I know, and a hot bath, more coffee and some food and I will also need my chaps as well as some fresh clothes. Tell Henry, he will know what to bring.'

'Straight thinking, Griff,' Philburgh said. 'I will give you a few pills to ease the hurt and some laudanum to carry just in case, but ride easy. A dead man cannot help the boy.'

I bathed and slept the night in the hotel, knowing that Laura was watching over me. After a hearty breakfast I dressed in the range clothes Henry Mendoza had brought in for me that morning and wearing a light-weight straw Stetson two sizes too big for me, Laura and I made our way along to the sheriff's office. Joe Sawyer was not there – worn out, the elderly lawman was still sleeping, as were the rest of the posse having spent well over forty-eight hours in the saddle. Billy Walking Horse was leaning against the thick door that led through to the cells and Mendoza was seated on the desk, both men were smoking raising a light haze of expelled tobacco smoke that drifted across the room and out of the open door. I carefully removed the hat and adjusted the soft cotton packing Mose the old storekeeper had kindly fitted to the inside of the sweat band so that it did not rub too hard on the uncovered wound, and dumped the gunny sack of supplies I had also purchased there.

I did not see any need to ask but felt that I should. 'We are going after the boy, Charlie Otis, you up for that, Billy? Henry will join us so that will be a posse of three, more would be a hindrance.'

'Sure, Boone, I will find them for you, you show me where the posse lost the trail.'

'Henry?'

'No need to ask, boss.'

'And I am going too,' Laura said quietly.

'No,' I turned to her. 'You will stay here, there is no way you can come.'

'He is my son, I have the right, Charlie is my responsibility,' Laura said, quietly, firmly.

'And the lives of these two men are mine,' I said. 'Worrying about your safety would jeopardize that, I would be thinking of you and not of them.'

'I can ride and I can shoot, you would not need to worry about me, I can do anything a man can do.' There was an edge of anger creeping into her soft voice.

'Can you piss standing up?' I said.

'What the hell has that got to do with anything?' Her face reddened.

'My point is that you cannot do everything a man can do, you have never been under gunfire and besides, you would be concerned for Chuck just as we are but you would put that concern before your own safety and likely the safety of the three of us.'

'Damn you,' she said, and stamped out of the room storm-faced with an anger I had not seen before, not even when I had first met her and Charlie out by the

118

broken wagon on Liberty Creek.

'You handled that well, boss,' Mendoza said sarcastically, stubbing out his cigarette.

I shrugged. 'I am right, it had to be said.'

'You sure you want me along, Boone?' Billy said. 'I can't always piss standing up either.'

I rolled my eyes and shook my head, turning away less they saw the hint of relief creeping on to my face. I opened the gun cabinet, selected a box of shells and a Winchester rifle, telling them to sort out weapons for themselves and meet me at the livery stable.

It was early afternoon when we reached the remains of the brush corral where the posse had lost the trail left by the fleeing outlaws. Mendoza and I loosened the cinches of our horses and squatted down, sharing my makings while Billy Walking Horse did his thing, which was mostly talking a lot to himself and walking around in an ever increasing circle. I dozed a little, hoping to chase away the beginnings of a returning headache. Eventually the old Indian returned, sat down and rolled himself a smoke from my tobacco. He was thinking and I knew from experience there was little point in trying to hurry him along. I waited.

'They had remounts here, fresh animals. The horses they rode here from town were beat and they went north with one rider, we will find them eventually if you want but there is little point in doing that. The fresh horses went east. I can pick up their trail but it will be slow going – the ground is hard and they cleared some of the tracks with brush.'

119

I did not ask how he knew, it was enough that he did.

'They have at least a full day on us,' Mendoza said. 'That is one long time.'

'I don't think they were in a hurry, they will feel safe for a while,' I said.

'Safe?'

'They were not pushing their animals, they have a plan and maybe another corral.'

'Anywhere that you can recall to hide out to the east?' I said, turning to Mendoza with the question.

'Mostly to the east of here is Will Rider's Rocking Jay, mostly open range when you are clear of the foothills, maybe a couple of line shacks back from the old days before he expanded.'

'And plenty of water,' I said.

'There is that too.'

'What are you thinking, Billy?'

'I know the country pretty good, Griff, Henry is right, a bunch could hide themselves for a long time in those hills.'

'I don't think so,' I said, with more confidence than I actually felt. 'They aimed to leave Liberty with a sack full of money and they would have wanted to get well clear and fast. They may well have another remuda waiting for them, maybe even two but my guess is their plan would have been to watch their back trail briefly and then head north for Montana and Canada or south to Colorado but I don't think they will be in the hurry they were planning on.'

'Why not?' Mendoza asked.

'They know a posse isn't going to beat its backsides

out over a mere $500.'

'But with the kid?' The old Indian frowned, the deep lines adding to the aging wrinkles of the seventy year old.

'They may well change their plan and hide out until things cool down, we need to check out those line shacks. It was one big mistake them taking the boy.'

'We'll find him, deputy,' Walking Horse said, taking a small can from his shoulder bag, opening it and sticking a chaw of dark chewing tobacco into his cheek and smiling at me.

'That's a filthy habit, Billy,' I said.

CHAPTER ELEVEN

RETRIBUTION

The bunch rode in a downcast silence on the fresh mounts gathered from the brush corral. Ben Logan was in a killing mood but he had to rein it in for a while, his main concern being the losing of the posse that had chased them from Liberty and then to getting the bunch clear of Wyoming Territory without attracting too much attention. Flynn and Treadwell brought up the rear, Flynn having trouble with the squirming boy, the kid crying and Flynn cursing him then watching as Treadwell moved closer and reaching over, swung the boy out from Flynn's arms and seated him on the front of his own saddle, telling him to hold hard on the pommel. Flynn glared but said nothing. It was a mess that would need sorting out swiftly; kidnapping children was not something any one of them would have considered and he doubted that Flynn would find any support for his careless action from any of the rest of the crew.

Close by to the line shack, Vargas broke away from the group and carefully skirted the cabin making sure their hideout had not been discovered. Satisfied, he waved from the yard and dismounted, dropping the pole gate so that the others could ride straight in. Flynn was the first to dismount, reaching up for the boy and half carrying, half dragging him to the cabin. Once inside he shoved the boy into a corner and whispered to him; the boy paled, his crying turned to a miserable sobbing which seemed to please Flynn but not Treadwell who sat down beside the child, ruffled his hair and tossed him a blanket to help still the shivering.

In the corral, Lomax finished his chores with the horses and went inside to light the stove while Vargas and Logan rolled smokes and anxiously watched the ridge for the returning Harris.

'It will take him a while yet,' Vargas said, firing his quirly, passing the makings to Logan. 'He will take the long way back. Smitty should be here first I guess.'

'If he got clear,' Logan said, shaking the dusty Durham tobacco on to a brown Rizla paper.

'You know Smitty, he blends in, probably offered to join the posse.'

Logan smiled at that, the thought of Howard Smith riding with a posse would be something to see. He relaxed, a little glad to be out of Flynn's company, wondering why the two of them should not just rest up the horses and then ride out together but knowing that was not possible. He had a responsibility to the bunch and for bringing Flynn into their company. 'Crap,' he said quietly, almost as if to himself. 'That goddamned Flynn,

123

what the hell is wrong with him?'

'Just about everything, *amigo*,' Vargas said.

'We can put this right,' Logan said.

'I do not think so, it cannot be undone.'

'What then?'

'He will not give up the boy, you will have to kill him for that to happen.'

'I know.'

'I'll back your play, I do not believe anyone will side with him, not even his partner.'

'Tomorrow then, before we move out.'

'You will take him down?'

'Yes, I will take him down and Jimmy Treadwell too if he does back him.'

'He won't.'

'I hope not, I like the kid, he just chose bad company, could happen to anyone,' Logan grinned. 'Look at you and me.'

The problem seemingly resolved on a high note, the pair dogged their smokes and were making their way to the cabin when a tired Tom Harris rode into the yard. Vargas took the man's lathered horse to the small lean-to and began to rub it down with a blanket.

'Any problems?' Logan asked.

'No, Ben, got a sore butt is all.'

'Come on inside, I'll get you some coffee, Chad has fired up the stove.'

'I know, I saw the smoke from the ridge,' Harris said.

'That's not good,' Logan said. 'We need to be careful, find some dry wood or eat cold rations tonight.'

'We'll find some dry wood,' Vargas said, joining them.

'I need hot coffee and a hot meal, we all do.'

Logan nodded and the three men made their way from the corral to the cabin where the rest of the crew were gathered around the table, looking at the small stack of bills set up in its centre. A smoke haze gathered silently above the heads of the hushed group.

'How did we do?' Flynn asked, ignoring the newcomers.

'Five hundred and some change,' Lomax said.

'Sonofabitch,' Harris said, 'that was our original stake.'

Flynn cursed.

'Shut your mouth in front of the boy,' Logan said quietly, bringing it to a head there and then. Stepping away from the table, his hand resting on the side of his holster, manipulating his long fingers, making his intention clear.

Flynn stared at the man long and hard, calculating, then his eyes shifted to Vargas leaning against the door frame, silhouetted by the setting sun. He relaxed, his hands clear of his Colt. He smiled. 'Crap, we broke even then.'

The tension in the room vanished almost as quickly as it had appeared. Lomax laughed and said, 'All we have to do now is ascertain who gets what.' There was a long pause then more laughter.

The men were halfway through a hot supper of sonofagun stew conjured up by Vargas when a tired Howard Smith rode into the yard. Treadwell, who had been sitting apart from the others trying to persuade the boy to eat, pushed his plate to one side and offered to stable the bay, an offer gladly accepted by the weary and dusty Smith.

'What did we leave behind?' Logan asked, when the man had eaten and consumed two cups of dark coffee.

'Well, for starters two bags of money.' Smith leaned back in his chair and pulled a crumpled stogie from his chequered vest pocket, firing it with a thumb-struck match.

'Casualties?' Logan said.

'The bank cashier peed his pants and the manager hurt his shoulder blowing a hole in the ceiling with a sawed off.'

'The badge?'

'He must have a head like a rock. Took the weight of two rounds to the noggin, both bounced off, left him with a couple of nifty scars and a headache he will never forget but he is one tough hombre and was just coming around when I lit out.'

'That all, Smitty?'

'No that isn't all, Ben, town is up in arms about the kid Flynn snatched.' He looked in the direction of the big man and then at the boy cowering in the corner. 'Boy's name is Charlie Otis, seems he is close to the deputy, the boy and his old lady both.'

'That's bad.'

'Sure enough is, Ben, they will haunt us and that boy to the ends of the earth, I doubt they are worried about the small change you stole but the boy, well that's a different matter.'

'You stupid sonofabitch, what the hell went down?'

126

Logan said, turning toward Flynn.

'He recognized me, what else could I have done?'

'You could have stayed put in the alley like I said.'

'You're through telling me what to do, Logan, the kid is my responsibility and I will deal with it. Come here, boy, now.' He took the boy by the arm and led him out into the darkness, followed closely by a worried-looking Treadwell. 'Me, Jimmy and Charlie here will be moving on come daylight, you don't like that you can go to hell, you and your greaser friend.' He did not close the door behind him.

'You going to take that, Ben?' Smith said.

'I will deal with it in the morning, I need to think.'

Charlie Otis was terrified but he was also strong; he had to be, so many bad thoughts and hard times had filled his young years and only recently had he begun to live the life a boy of his age should. Fishing, riding a fine horse, making a real Crow Indian his friend, seeing his mother happy and, above all, the certainty that Griffin Boone would never let anything bad happen to him. He had promised that. Seeing the deputy on the ground with a bloody head had shattered those dreams now, though hearing he was alive, Charlie Otis knew the lawman would find him and that anticipation kept him awake most of the night, curled up warm under the blankets the man called Jimmy had wrapped around him.

It was barely daylight when the shadow of Huck Flynn towered above him. 'Take a pee, boy, eat this and be ready to ride in ten.' He tossed a couple of strips of

127

jerked beef on to his lap and turned away, moving across the lean-to and kicking the booted feet of the still sleeping Jimmy Treadwell. 'Get ready to light out, kid, we've got better places to be. I'll saddle the horses, be ready to ride when I get back.'

Charlie watched carefully as the big man moved to the small workbench, picked up a pair of saddle bags and swung them across his broad shoulders.

'Why are we taking the boy, Huck?' Treadwell said.

'Insurance – the posse crowds us, the boy gets it – country bumpkins, they will understand that.'

'I don't think so, Huck, let's send him home or leave him here, Ben will take care of him.'

'You disagreeing with me, Jimmy boy?'

'I guess so.'

'And if I tell you to go to hell?'

'Maybe I'll go there then and just maybe I will take you with me.'

'You stupid green kid,' Flynn said, pulling his Colt and punching a fast round into Jimmy Treadwell's chest, the weight of the round knocking him back against the timber-framed doorway. But the kid wasn't finished and as he fell, he pulled and fired; a lucky round perhaps but good enough to stop Flynn, hitting him a half inch above the bridge of his swollen nose, snapping his head back and sending him sprawling backwards across and upon the small bench.

At the first round Charlie dived under the table and then as Flynn's blood dripped through a crack in the aged timber, he rolled out from under, ran for the door and into the arms of Ben Logan.

*

Logan rolled out of his blankets just after the first rays of a promising sunlit day filtered its way through the dusty, fly-speckled windows of the cabin. He set his hat on his head and pulled on one of his boots; he had slept in his pants having the deep-rooted outlaw fear of being rousted by a posse wearing only his long johns. Vargas was already at the stove when the two shots sounding almost as one cracked across the yard.

'What the hell?' Logan said, moving quickly across the boarded floor with one boot on and the other in his hand.

'The lean-to,' Vargas said, drawing his gun and moving swiftly in the direction of the ringing silence that always seems to follow the echo of gunfire.

Logan hobbled after him reaching for his own sidearm and finding he had not strapped it on. He reached the open doorway just as Charlie Otis, wide-eyed and white-faced, rushed out to him, grabbing him. Logan held the boy close making soothing noises, the way he would to a frightened horse. 'Easy, boy, I've got you, easy, easy now.'

Vargas stepped out of the lean-to closing the door behind him and holstering his weapon, looking first at the boy and then at Logan, saying quietly, 'Looks like a shoot-out that nobody won.'

'Flynn?'

'Deader than a hat, round took him just over that big nose, dead centre.'

'Jimmy Treadwell?'

'Looks dead to me, round hit him in the breast.'

'Goddamn,' Logan said, then looking at the boy and turning away from the lean-to, he headed back toward the cabin walking straight past the curious Howard Smith and Tom Harris as they emerged bleary-eyed from a restless night. 'Flynn was a hole in the road but the kid seemed OK.'

'They are both OK now I guess,' Vargas said, then watching as Logan and the boy entered the cabin, hung back to explain to Harris and Smith what he had seen in the lean-to.

'Flynn was a real piece of crap, but I liked the kid,' Smith said.

'I wonder what went down,' Harris mused.

'I guess we'll never know,' Smith said.

'The kid see it?' Harris asked.

'You want to ask him that?' Vargas answered curtly.

'No I do not,' Harris said, heading for the outhouse at the back of the barn.

Following a quick and silent breakfast, Logan left Charlie Otis in the care of Howard Smith, who was known to have had children of his own in New Orleans and, taking Vargas aside said, 'We have to move and we have to get that kid back to Liberty, you have any ideas as to just how we do that, Emilio?'

'You are right, *amigo*, that posse will never give up all the time we have the boy, they may not worry about the small change but like I said earlier the kid is another matter.'

'The only way I see it happening is to set him on a horse and one of us head him back toward town, take the long way round in case they are smart enough to back track us. Maybe head him for the Overland Stage trail.'

'Something like that, there are bound to be riders out searching.'

'And several homesteads along the way,' Logan said.

'You think he would be safe?'

'Get Harris to sort him out a gentle mount, give him a canteen and take him as far we dare.'

'Then head back for Glory and split as we intended,' Vargas said, then added as an afterthought, 'Five hundred dollars will not get us far. That Flynn was a real piece of work, a complete fuck-up, without him we would be free and clear with money in our saddlebags.'

'Let's get it done then,' Logan said, a deep weariness in his voice. 'I'll talk to the men, you see to Harris and a horse.'

'Who is going to take him?'

'Smith, if he does run into trouble he can always claim to have been out searching for the kid.'

'The boy will talk.'

'There is that, but not right off and Smitty is resourceful.'

'Smith it is then.'

Howard Smith did indeed have two children of his own and a lovely wife in New Orleans; he had it in his mind to head back for Louisiana just as soon as he had seen Charlie Otis on to a safe trail to Liberty. Smith had no intention of going back to Glory, that would be pure folly. He had taken Seymour Hodge for well over what he was due from a share out of the $500 and there was no need to say goodbye to Logan or Vargas – chances were their trails would cross again somewhere down the line. No, the smart move was to unload the kid and head south as fast as he could.

Charlie Otis rode quietly beside Smith, a little figure on a big horse. He liked Smith, felt comfortable with the tall man in the chequered suit, he had seen him around town and people seemed to like him. For his part Smith kept up a quiet chatter, reassuring the boy that he would be home with his mother very likely before nightfall and that his friend the deputy was well and just a walking wounded lawman.

'He took a couple of knocks but when I last saw him he was feisty and raring to come looking for you, wouldn't surprise me one bit we didn't meet him on the trail hereabouts and I would be obliged if you did not mention my being at that cabin with those outlaws, I was only passing by but you know how people think.'

Charlie had no idea what grown-up people thought but his young life had been such a whirlwind of change since the meeting with the ugly man they called Flynn and Jimmy the boy who rode with him, that very little made any real sense to him, not even the shooting, the roar of the pistols and the two men down and dead. No, if Mr Smith did not want to mention him being at the cabin that was fine by Charlie Otis, just so long as he was back with his mother and Griffin Boone.

Just a little after noon, Smith saw the dust of two or three riders heading their way. It was too late to run and too many to fight, so he played out the hand he was dealt, hailing the riders from the small ridge and recognizing the deputy, he hurried their horses towards them, yelling and waving at the top of his voice.

CHAPTER TWELVE

HARD RIDE
TO GLORY

My head hurt like hell, I had taken all of the little pills
Doc Philburg had given me and I was reluctant to take
any more of the laudanum. We had been riding all
morning mostly in silence, stopping frequently for Billy
Walking Horse to dismount and study the ground,
always leaving a dark gob of tobacco-stained spit like a
wolf marking his trail then spitting again in the direction we should take. It was a hard ride and I felt about
done in.

An hour later I was half asleep in the saddle when
Billy Walking Horse raised a hand to shield his eyes
from the sun saying, 'Riders coming, two of them, one
looks like. . . .' His words were drowned by the hoof
beats as I pushed the mare forward at speed to meet the
two riders, one I had already spotted was Charlie, the

other was the investor who had taken Seymour Hodge for a roll in the Black Pony and was looking for a barbering business in Liberty. Charlie leaped from the saddle and ran toward me, I grabbed him, swung him in the air and held him close to me. His arms were around my neck and I realized that it was the first time I had actually held him close. His eyes were flooding, as were mine.

'Thanks be to God I found you, I've been riding round in circles most of the morning then found Charlie here by an old line camp or whatever you call them,' Smith said, shaking hands with Mendoza and a puzzled Walking Horse.

'What the heck are you doing out here on your own, Mr Smith?' Henry said.

'I got separated from the posse last night, couldn't find my way back and suddenly it was dark. Didn't anyone miss me? I've been stuck out here in this godforsaken wilderness all night, found the kid wandering around this morning and neither of us knew the way home.'

I hugged the boy and wiped away his tears with my bandanna. 'Hush now, Charlie, you will be home in a little while, your mom is waiting. Henry, you take Chuck and Mr Smith here back to Liberty with you, Billy and I will carry on, maybe back track these two and find that cabin.'

'Can't you come with us, sir?' There was the hint of panic in Charlie's voice.

'No, Charlie, but I will be along directly.'

'They shoot each other, they are mean men at the

cabin, most of them.'

'I will be OK, Billy will take care of me.'

'What will I tell Mom?'

'You be sure to tell her I love her, son, you just tell her that. Thank you, sir,' I said, turning to Smith. 'Thank you for finding the boy and trying to get him home. I'll see you back in town in a day or so, we will drink on it.'

'We surely will,' Smith said.

'Take care, Henry,' I said.

'You too, boss,' he said, reining his mount around, picking up Charlie's leading rein and I watched as the three of them headed in the direction of Liberty, seven miles to the west.

Billy and I watched them out of sight, the sense of relief in me was beyond anything I had ever felt in my life before, it was as if a gigantic weight I had not realized was there had been lifted from my shoulders and its departure had brought about a realization of the great responsibility I had taken upon myself with Laura and Charlie. It was a realization and I welcomed it, the dawning of a new day. The headache subsided, my leg no longer pained me and the morning seemed a whole lot brighter. 'Let's ride, Billy,' I said. 'Let us end this as quickly as possible. I need to go home.'

I studied the place long and hard through my army field glasses. It was run-down and unused but there was a whisp of smoke leaking from the metal stack and the faint smell of fresh wood smoke. The corral was empty but there were plenty of signs to show that it had recently been used. We watched for nearly an hour but there was no movement; once a deer wandered through the yard, the animal appeared to be in no hurry or in any way disturbed.

'Clear, Billy, but cover me with that old Henry of yours just in case.' He nodded and spat, climbed down and levered a shell into its breech.

The mare picked her way down the incline and, nearing the cabin, I drew my piece and rested it on my thigh but there was no need, the place was deserted. I climbed down and quickly checked the cabin and then the lean-to, pushing open the door, smelling the stink of blood and hearing the crazy buzzing of the gorged blue-bottle flies. There were two men, the same two men I had first encountered down by Liberty Creek when Laura's wagon had thrown a wheel. Flynn, the older of the two and the most wanted was on his back, spread over the narrow bench; he had been shot in the head just above his big nose. His pistol was near his hand and it had been fired. The single round, I assumed, was the one that done for his sidekick, the kid called Jimmy Treadwell. I picked up Flynn's piece and walked over to the boy and was startled when his eyelids flickered and slowly opened. Kneeling down, I swished the flies away from his mouth, watching as very slowly his eyes half opened and began to focus on me. I nursed his head and wiped the blood from his lips with my bandanna. The wound in his chest was fatal, of that there was no doubt, just above the heart – why he was still alive I had no idea.

'Hang on, kid,' I said. 'Let me get my canteen.'

He held my hand and shook his head, only a slight

137

movement but enough to pump a fresh gout of blood from the bullet wound. His lips moved and I leaned down to hear his last whispered words, a question.

'Is Charlie safe, Sheriff?'

'Home with his mama by now I would guess.'

'That's good enough,' he said, 'and me too, home with mine. . . .' He sighed and died with just the hint of a smile on his bloody lips.

'You want we should bury them, Boone?' Billy Walking Horse said, his big shadow blotting out the sun which tried so hard to lighten the darkness of the lean-to's interior.

'This one, yes, but leave the other one to the wolves.'

We rolled the kid into a shallow grave, dug with a shovel we found in the corral, Billy filled it in and rolled a couple of rocks on to the mound. 'You want to say something godly over him?'

'No, I don't know anything godly, Billy. You can if you feel the need, your god will do just as well.'

While Billy got the stove going again I poked about the cabin, which looked like it had been the home for several days of a group of at least five or six men. They had left little to tell of their passing but I did find a small sheaf of wanted fliers left behind in their haste and among those was one of a Ben Logan and a Howard J. Smith, both late of New Orleans. I showed it to Billy, he smiled and said, 'I guess you will not be buying him that drink after all, Boone.'

'He's long gone on his way to Louisiana by now would be my guess,' I said.

'I'll bet he don't stop till he gets there,' Billy said.

'With the several hundred dollars he took off Seymour Hodge.'

'Luck of the devil, he surely is a winner.'

'Charlie liked him so he can't be all bad,' I said.

'Nobody ever is, Boone, well hardly anyone that is – maybe except that pile of crap in the lean-to.'

Darkness was fast approaching and we knew Billy would not be able to find the outlaws' trail, so we opted to spend the night in the line shack and cook the last of our supplies for a supper that neither of us really felt like eating.

'You bring a jug, Billy?' I said.

'Just a little one,' he said.

'Go fetch it.'

'Yes, sir.'

The following morning we awoke to a thunder and rain storm. The thunder was directly overhead and the lightning that preceeded each roar danced about in the low hills at the back of the cabin, one striking the large cottonwood standing close by the lean-to, sending a burst of flame skywards and leaving the tree smoking. Billy Walking Horse did not like thunder and lightning; he moved away from the window and opened the door. I could smell the burning sulphur.

I moved to his side, opening the door wider and staring out at the smoking cottonwood. 'You think that was the Devil calling for Huck Flynn's soul, Billy?' I said.

'Damned if I know but I sure hope it wasn't aimed at me.'

'It will pass, I see the sky clearing to the south and I

have a feeling that is the direction we will be headed.'

'You think?'

'Yes, I think.'

'This storm is going to make their trail hard to find, the rain is washing any sign away.'

'They will keep a while.'

'You want to ride in the rain? We can if you are of a mind to,' Billy said.

'No I do not,' I said. 'I don't want to get wet and stay wet all day and neither do I want to end up like that cottonwood tree. We will sit it out.'

'You got any smokes left?'

'A couple.' I passed him a cheroot.

'Filthy habit,' he said.

It took Billy Walking Horse the Crow Indian less than an hour to pick up the hidden trail left by the departing outlaws. It led south as I had expected. 'We can save a hell of a lot of time here, Billy, we'll head for Glory – that's where I think they are heading. Maybe they have fresh mounts there or assume we would not consider it as a hideout.'

'It's a risk,' Billy said.

'One I will take,' I said.

'You got no jurisdiction down there,' Billy argued.

'I don't think Gus Winters will object, do you?'

'I guess not.'

'Then pick us out the quickest trail. I want to be there well before evening.'

'It's a hard ride, Boone.'

'Then we will ride hard, Billy.'

CHAPTER THIRTEEN

BULLETS AND BADMEN

Logan was tired, more than tired – he was weary to the bone. He sat his mount half asleep, pushing on to Glory, the head of a bunch that were as poor today as they were yesterday and now pursued by a man with a badge, no doubt intent on their utter destruction. The whole deal – the planning, the gathering of the men from New Orleans to Wyoming Territory – was a waste and all because of one man. He hated Huck Flynn with a passion and suffered the irritation of knowing that the hate could never be satisfied, Jimmy Treadwell had robbed him of that one chance. Emilio Vargas was more matter of fact about the events at the line camp which, by his simple reckoning, had turned out well and the kid had saved either he or Logan the job of killing Flynn.

Exactly what had gone down in the lean-to he had no idea, but guessed it was about the boy Charlie Otis. Either Flynn had harmed him or Treadwell thought it likely that he would and had tried to end it there. A lucky shot, it had to have been; the kid was no match for Flynn, of that he was certain. Just as certain as he was of the fact that sometimes it was the lucky shot that won the day, it had often been that way in the war and the way it always would be with guns. A brass round rolls off the loading line in a Connecticut factory, and along with thousands of others it gets boxed and shipped west, it ends up in a store, a man buys a box and loads his gun. Out of all of the thousands and thousands of .45 calibre rounds, that one single bullet is fired by a green kid, maybe as he is going down under another man's gun, and it hits that other man smack bang in the head. A wild, lucky round for neither of the two men. A lead bullet all the way from a factory in Hartford, Connecticut to the cylinder of a six gun in Wyoming Territory, never blessed, counted or tried, a totally anonymous lead projectile exploding from a brass casing and ending the life of Huck Flynn. And what of the round Flynn had fired, was that from the same box? Logan's thoughts wandered. 'Hey, *amigo*.' Vargas' voice shattered his reverie. 'You sleep, you fall, keep awake – we are nearly there, I'll cook us a meal to remember,' he laughed, 'or perhaps maybe one to forget.'

They were too worn out to check the town, they rode right on in, dismounting and leaving the care of the animals to Harris who took them to the corral by the run-down livery stable and tended their needs before his own. Like his friend Lomax, Harris was a killer who enjoyed the power of the six gun, the pleasure of it, but around horses he was as gentle as a lamb, talking to them, always feeding them before taking his own meal.

Vargas fired up the stove and got the coffee going, knowing it was what the men most needed. The food they had left was not really adequate but would have to do, a boiling pot and everything thrown in with herbs and wild onions for flavour, trail grub, it would be eaten and accepted by hungry men and then in the morning with a few dollars in their pokes they would split and, he guessed, head as far and as fast as they could clear of Wyoming Territory with little thought of food on their minds.

Logan belched loudly and pushed his plate to one side, then going behind the bar and coming out with a jug he had stashed for a celebratory occasion, the sharing of the money and hitting the trail north, east, west or in his and Vargas' case, south to Louisiana and the river, the big game. Now the dream was gone and the moonshine was just another drink to keep out the cold of a starless night. He would let Harris and Lomax go their own ways while he and the Mexican would have to find their gambling money elsewhere – or would they? He had to face up to it, he really wasn't much of an outlaw, he had been lieutenant in the army, it was an organized command supervised by others who in their turn were under the eye of a brigade commander, layer upon layer of authority to take the fall should things go awry, but with the bunch it was all down to him. He was responsible for the whole sorry mess, no higher command to take the heat if things went wrong. The hell with it, he thought, it just wasn't worth it. He would talk to Vargas about it in the morning although he knew the man would not agree and that they too would ride different trails away from Glory. Vargas to ply his trade with the cards and the Colt while he would try to make a legitimate life somewhere down the line. How hard could it be? All he had to do was get clear of the badge dogging their back trail and head north for Montana and Canada.

After supper, he joined Vargas on the porch wondering how or where to begin. He was a direct man so he followed that instinct. 'We need to talk, Emilio.'

The Mexican handed him a half smoked stogie and held a match to it for him. 'I know,' he said.

'I have simply had enough of the running, compadre, I need to rest, settle somewhere and grow old. I'm just not cut out to be a Black Bart and too old to be a Billy Bonney.'

'Good luck with that, Ben, sorry to ride on without you but whatever is best for you is best for me. I enjoyed the journey.'

Logan was both surprised and grateful. He stuck out his hand and Vargas took it, held it firmly, turned and went back into the dimly lit Glory Hole.

The bunch slept late the next morning having decided to ride clear of Glory in the afternoon, Harris and Lomax riding east together while he and Vargas went their very separate ways, Logan to Canada and the Mexican unhappy at the split but determined to head back to New Orleans. They ate the remains of the evening's meal in silence, each with a little over a hundred dollars in their pokes and a bundle of misery and disappointment on their minds. They did not blame Logan but heaped all of their hate on the late Huck Flynn.

CHAPTER FOURTEEN

EMPTY SADDLES

We sat our horses for a long while on the narrow trail overlooking the dead and gone township of Glory. Billy Walking Horse quietly chewing his tobacco and me drawing in the smoke from the last of my store-bought smokes. Glory looked forlorn in the late afternoon light, a slight breeze moved the tumbleweeds around the street and stirred the rusting windmill that fed the leaking water tank but that was all. The five horses in the corral stood heads down, weary and hot, tails swishing continuously at the troublesome flies. A whisper of smoke emitted from the metal chimney that stood erect against the far, bleached wooden side wall of the Glory Hole Saloon.

'What you thinking, Boone?' Billy said.

'I'm thinking they are in the saloon feeling safe and

drinking coffee,' I said.

'Maybe yes and maybe no, I thought I saw movement through the window of the hardware building across the street. Maybe a lookout. A Sioux move, a move they learned from the Crow, a move we learned from the birds, always leave a lookout.'

'Either way, sitting here isn't going to help.'

'You thinking of going down there?'

'You have a better idea?'

'Going down there, riding right into their guns is not an idea. Why not let me keep watch while you ride to Sioux Falls and get help? It's their county.'

'That would take too long, they could be gone by the time we got back.'

'A better plan then, I ride to Sioux Falls while you keep watch.'

'Same plan.'

'I'm tired, I don't want to spend my days watching over a ghost town, I want to go home,' Billy said. 'How many you think are down there anyways?'

'Six men robbed the bank, two we know for sure are dead, my guess is four.'

'So one spare horse.'

'You still sharp with that old .44 Henry of yours, Billy?'

'What are you thinking now?'

'I'm still thinking they are in there drinking coffee and we are up here talking about it.'

'So?'

'So I am going to ride down there and if you are right and there is a lookout, I will need you to back me up.

147

What's the range, maybe if you slide down the hill some you can make it 200, 220 yards? You up for that if the shooting starts?'

I watched as Billy slipped the brass framed long gun out of the saddle boot and checked the leaf sights. 'I can do that, I got fourteen rounds here, one of them is bound to hit.' He smiled. 'Don't you think?'

'If anyone, other than me, appears on the street you put a hard round through that tin bucket sitting there on the sidewalk under where that hardware store sign is hanging down. Can you see that?' I passed him the field glasses but he shook his head, half closed his obsidian black eyes, studied the deserted street and said, 'I got it.'

'Move down the hill a little then, if this goes south and there is gunfire and I go down you get the hell out of here and head back to Liberty. You got that, Billy?'

'I got my end, Boone, you just going to ride down there, walk in and arrest them?'

'Something like that, you take care of yourself, Billy,' I said, and I touched the mare's flank with my heels.

I did not hurry, the surefooted animal picked her way down the rocky slope and I sat her easy, pausing only once to remove the county badge from my shirt front and pinning it on to my vest, I wanted them to be in no doubt as to who I was. Passing the hardware store I thought I saw movement inside, a stirring of dust, the creaking of a floorboard and guessed that Billy Walking Horse was correct in his assumption that the building was occupied. I could see that the metal bucket already had a rusting bullet hole in its side, target practice for a some long-ago bored cowboy I supposed.

148

I reined the mare to a halt, slowly dismounted, looped the leathers across the broken hitching rail, took a deep breath and letting it out slowly pushed open the creaking, rotted batwing doors. I didn't expect a hail of lead to greet me figuring the outlaws would be curious and maybe even a little concerned at my seemingly untroubled appearance. At least that was what I was counting upon.

The room was dusty, the stink of stale tobacco, stale clothing on unwashed bodies laced with the smell of burned coffee. The furniture, what there was of it, was arranged much as I had left it following the discovery of Gus Winters' bloody gunshot body. There were three men in the centre of the room, two I recognized immediately from the fliers as Emilio Vargas the Mexican and the gunman Chad Lomax. The third man, tall, and handsome in a classical way, the sharp clean-cut features outlined by several days of rich red beard, was leaning against the bar.

'Gents,' I said, moving to the rough bar and setting my hip against it with all three men in clear sight, 'it is one hell of a hot afternoon, you have anything to drink around here?'

'Help yourself, sheriff,' the tall man said, noting the badge and nodding his head toward where a jug and a couple of preserve jars were set on the dusty rough pine surface of the bar. 'Only a jar, nothing fancy around here.'

I poured myself a drink with my left hand and raised the glass. 'Salud.'

'You on the job, sheriff, or just passing through?' the

tall man said.

It was a casual enough question asked in a friendly enough manner. I kept my eye on the Mexican, figuring that would be where the trouble came from should I wrong-foot the situation. 'On the clock, Ben, been on it for seven days in a row.'

'You know my name, how?' Logan said, his voice still calm and friendly.

'You left a flier at the line camp, it was a great help.' I shifted my gaze to the Mexican. 'You must be Emilio Vargas, the gunfighter, and you . . .' I nodded to where the third man was fidgeting, shuffling his small feet, 'you must be Chad Lomax, so many aliases I cannot recall them all.'

'And you are here for what?' Logan said, a hard edge creeping into his smooth voice.

'I'm here for you three, maybe four counting the man I assume to be Harris in the old hardware store across the street,' I said.

'You've got a lot of balls coming in here alone, sheriff,' Logan said.

'Actually I'm only a part-time deputy, usually I sit behind a desk in Liberty shuffling papers and only then when the elected man is out hunting people like you, but he has a bad cold and his wife kept him in bed, said she did not want him shooting any outlaws today. Oh, and I am not alone, got marksmen all around, they want to kill you but I want to take you in alive.'

'Check out the street, Chad, I think he is bluffing,' Vargas said.

'Your call,' I said.

Lomax cautiously pushed one of the batwing doors open, poked his head out and immediately the tin bucket on the far side of the street shot into the air, the clang of the bullet strike followed almost immediately by the crack of a distant rifle. The falling bucket never reached the ground before another shot sent it skywards again then a third and a fourth, the fifth round sending the bucket out of sight beneath the boardwalk. I had to smile, Billy Walking Horse showing me what an old man could do with a Henry rifle at over 200 yards. No sooner had the bucket wedged itself under the boards than a man broke cover from the old hardware store, only to go down halfway across as a round took him in the chest. Billy again having my back.

A white-faced, wild-eyed Lomax dived back inside the Glory Hole, his pistol in his hand as was mine. Vargas and Logan froze and I shot Lomax in the head as Vargas drew down on me and fired once, but I was already on the move firing at him and then twice at Logan, the second shot greeted by a yell of pain. The two men vanished through the doorway behind the bar and a great silence fell upon the room, that dreadful stillness that always follows a gunfight, concussed eardrums ringing, drowning out the echo, eyes running and the stink of the black powder smoke filling the nostrils. I opened the loading gate of my Colt and shook out the empty brass, reloading as I dashed to the entrance and out into the street, stepping over Harris the dead horse thief, hoping that Billy would recognize me and not give me the tin bucket treatment.

The nearest building of any substance was the old

livery stable next to the pole corral. I figured that was where the pair had holed up. I skirted the building and approached the open doors. Ever the gunfighter, Emilio Vargas stepped out, his gun holstered, dime novel west.

'Don't make me kill you, Vargas,' I said.

My gun was in my hand and I had no intention of holstering it and trying to out-pull him; he went for the piece but he never had a chance and perhaps he knew it. My gun already out and cocked, I dropped the hammer even as his gun was clearing the top of his holster and firing – he was very fast, the bullet striking me in the lower left thigh. The heavy round from my Colt drove him back into one of the uprights of the pole corral. Dying but still on his feet, he tried to raise the gun and as it came level I fired again. The bullet half turned him around and he dropped the gun. Somehow he found the strength to turn and face me, a half smile on his face, the white teeth stained with his blood as the punctured lungs tried and failed to give him air. 'Hey, gringo,' was all he said as his legs gave way and he fell backwards against the rails, slowly sliding down.

I holstered my Colt; Logan wasn't thought of as a gunfighter.

I waited and moments later he emerged from the deep shadow of the barn and into the bright sunlight, moving to his left as he did so, getting the late afternoon sun to his back and into my eyes; that was his edge. His gun was also holstered and his hand hung loose beside it, the bottom of his left pants leg was dark with blood, at least one of my rounds had scored a hit. He looked across toward the body of Emilio Vargas, the man on his back, his arms wide stretched and spread across the lowest rail of the corral, his chin on his chest, his dead eyes staring at his dusty boots but seeing only the big nowhere. Logan returned his gaze to me, the pale blue eyes heavy lidded with pain or sadness, I had no way of knowing which. 'He was a good man, a good friend,' he said quietly.

'He was a gunfighter, a killer of men,' I said.

'Are you not a killer of men, Boone? Have you not killed men here or in battle?'

'I gave him a choice,' I said.

'One you knew he would not take.'

'That is a moot point,' I said.

'A moot point? That one would have puzzled Lomax.'

'Excuse me?'

'No matter,' he said. 'What now?'

'Now you also have that choice to make.'

'Looks like we both took a hit. Emilio tag you?' he said.

'Just about.' I looked down at my own bloody leg, feeling my left foot moist in my boot.

'Five men dead for a lousy $500,' Logan said.

'It wasn't about the money,' I said.

'The lawmen that were killed here?'

I shook my head.

'Flynn and Vargas killed them, I couldn't stop it.'

'And not about them either,' I said.

'The boy?'

'Yes, the boy.'

'That was Flynn again and his partner did for him.'

153

'I know, we left Flynn for the wolves but we buried the kid.'

'I'm glad of that.'

'You were in the war?' he said, changing the subject, watching for movement over my shoulder up to the rise, where he guessed the shot that killed Harris came from.

'A lot of people were,' I said.

'I hear you served with the Confederacy, a Johnny Reb, I heard of you some place.'

'You heard right then,' I said, opening the long jacket clear of my holstered Colt.

'You were with John Bell Hood at Nashville?'

'I was.'

'We sure enough whipped your rebel asses there, didn't we?'

'That is how it got written up but you couldn't finish it there, you couldn't finish it on the Granny White Pike and you cannot finish it here.'

'We would have if'n Confederates had not blown the Duck River Crossing. Were you there as well?'

'I was one of the last men across, it was raining.'

'It's a small world, Boone. Weird how the war comes around and around like a circle, a snake biting its own tail.'

'Some things we have no control over, Logan, there are things we do not and probably never will understand about that war.'

'I've robbed a lot of banks, but I never killed anyone,' he said.

'That was sweet of you,' I said.

'You think you can out pull me?'

154

'I know I can so let's get it done,' I said, thinking why, why get it done, what was the point, just another body to bury, his or mine? I let my coat fall back across my holster and stuffed my hands deep into the pockets.

'Mount up, Logan, ride out of here and never come back to Wyoming Territory, you do and I will kill you.' I turned and limped across the open ground to the front of the Glory Hole, where the mare was shaking her head and pawing impatiently at the ground with a front hoof, disturbed by the exchange of gunfire. I rubbed her muzzle and raised my bloody leg, finding the stirrup and swinging up on to her back. I turned her head back towards Logan and stared down at him.

'Before you leave, bury your dead and loose those horses.'

'Why are you doing this?' Logan said.

'Why not?' I said, tossing the words over my shoulder as I turned the mare's head toward the approaching Billy Walking Horse, the open range and home. 'Why the hell not?'

The following afternoon after a long soak in the warm spring, Laura tended to my wounded leg, changing the dressing of the previous night hastily applied upon my return to Arrowhead. The wound inflicted by Emilio Vargas as he fell dying in the broken down corral back in Glory had bled far worse than the actual damage appeared to warrant. The bullet had passed cleanly through the fleshy part of my thigh and although it was painful and had initially bled profusely it was not as bad as I had thought, missing the bone and leaving a small

.45 calibre hole on one side and a slightly larger and ragged wound on the other. She lingered over the dressing, her slim fingers gently tracing the ancient, ragged webs of grey scar tissue on my right leg, my own private legacy from the Battle of Nashville.

'Are you a God-fearing man, Griffin Boone?' Laura asked.

'I could not believe in any god I was afraid of,' I said.

'Do you not believe in God, then?'

'Not an actual god, no, I do not think that I do but I do believe in a Higher Power, a universal order of sorts.'

She leaned down and gently kissed the old wounds. She sighed deeply and said, 'He did fine work that man of mine and we must always be grateful for that.' Then she looked at me and smiled at my confusion. 'When you were shot in the head, you were delirious for hours, ranting, praising, weeping, we were alone, I believe you told me just about everything of any importance that has ever happened to you.'

I tried to sit up, embarrassed, I opened my mouth to speak, although I had no idea of what to say but she leaned forward and kissed my mouth, silencing me.

'Shush, cowboy, we have a life together, a chance at a great happiness my God or your Higher Power has made possible for us. We will make the most of it.'

And then she was in my arms, weeping for joy and for sadness, a moist mixture of both as it was for both of us.

EPILOGUE

It was a fine Wyoming late morning, the near midday sun warmed me and the inaction tempted me into rolling my second cigarette of the day. Forsaking cheroots and smoking Durham in the mornings was a newly acquired habit, that and sitting there on Arrowhead's veranda, my aching leg resting on a footstool. Henry had driven Laura and Chuck into Liberty, his mother and I both felt it necessary to show the boy there was nothing more to be frightened of, understanding as we did the shock he must have had on the day of the bank robbery and the subsequent events leading to his release. I was still too sore in the leg to ride a horse, yet alone a bouncing buckboard. I shook the dusty makings from the Durham sack and closed the tab with my teeth; it was an old but not forgotten familiar act. I rolled the loose tobacco into a slim brown quirly and fired it, letting the raw smoke out very slowly whilst watching the buckboard coming down the rise and into the front yard. I recognized the slim hunched-up figure of Heck Thomas behind the two-horse team and noted that the

157

flatbed of the buckboard was piled high with packing cases, trunks and small items of furniture including the old man's rocking chair. He pulled to a halt in front of me, careful not to make too much of a dust cloud and whatever little there was quickly drifted away on the warm morning breeze.

'I heard you went and got yourself shot.' He nodded to the propped-up leg.

'You heard right, Heck.'

'It hurt much?'

'Some.'

'Same leg as took them balls in Nashville?'

'No, that leg was full so I started on the other one.'

'Mind if I step down?'

'You are always welcome here, Heck, you know that,' I said.

'I know it but it's polite to ask.' He climbed down, creaking a little more than usual I fancied. He stamped both feet hard on the ground to get the circulation moving, a buckboard seat can be pretty hard on the backside and would even leave a young man with numb legs after a while. He grunted to himself and fished under the seat, coming up with a brown manila envelope and a jug of 'shine. Mounting the wood-boarded veranda, he set both down on the small table beside me. 'A very special brew, you got any glasses handy?'

'Bit early in the day for me but you help yourself.'

He vanished inside, returning seconds later carrying two china mugs. 'These will have to do, can't see any damned glasses.' He set them beside the jug and pushed the envelope across to me.

'You want to sit down?' I asked, picking up the envelope.

'Go ahead, Griff, open it,' he said quietly, still standing his ground.

I opened the envelope and pulled out a small sheaf of papers and quickly examined them. The deeds to the Half Moon and a bill of sale signed by him with a space next to my scrawled name in uneven capitals, still empty.

'What is this all about, Heck?'

'Bill of sale for the Half Moon at the last price you offered me if it still holds good.'

'It does but what brought this on?'

'Big grizz in my front yard yesterday looked at me cross-eyed, sizing me up, he was sure enough a mean one and I figured it was time to move on.'

'Grizzlies very rarely come down this low, Heck, and not ever in summer, you know that.'

'Grizz or not, it was a big sonofabitch and I do not want him or her chewing on my bones. You want the Moon or not? Just say.'

'Of course I do, I will get the papers filed in town and the money paid into your account as soon as I can ride.'

'One other thing, I want to stay here with you until I head out for that last roundup, that OK with you? I can pay my keep out of the money you pay for the Moon – oh, and you can pay the late tax I owe out of that as well.'

'You are welcome to stay, there is a small cabin out back of the main bunkhouse where come roundup I sometimes put up part-time drovers. I will ask Maria to get it ready for you.'

'That would suit me just fine, and Billy Walking Horse can spend drinking time with me?'

'Sure, when do you want to move in?'

'Now, today, I think I just did.' He looked relieved, smiling happily as he poured the potent white liquid into the mugs and handing one to me before sitting on the spare seat. 'Here's how, Griffin Boone, here's how.'

We drank a while that sunny afternoon, Heck Thomas relieved to be free from the real or imagined bear and my head filled with happy thoughts of Laura and the boy who would soon be home. I would give her the Half Moon, both as a wedding present and as the security she both longed for and deserved. It was a sure enough fine day all around.